HAUNTED HOME?

"*SummerHome in Fenton, NY. On the outside, it resembles a typical retirement community. Inside, however, SummerHome could be the haunt of a murdering poltergeist.*" *JD said as he and Elaine walked around the apartment. Sam followed them with the camera.* "*In one week, a trio of deaths has left the staff and residents numb. Add to this rumors of other ghostly apparitions making appearances within these sterile halls and you will ask yourself, 'Is SummerHome the lair of a deadly paranormal entity? And if so, why, who is it, and how do we exercise it from the premises?' Well, the NE-PAT team is here to answer all of these questions for you. Join us now, why don't you, for one of the scariest investigations to date as we enter the haunted nursing home on this episode of Para-Hunters! CUT!*" *JD declared, and Sam turned off the camera.*

SummerHome

SECOND EDITION
© 2022 by Thomas R Clark
Published By St. Rooster Books
Cover art © 2021 Lynne Hansen
Inlay Designs © 2022 Thomas R Clark & © 2023 Deborah Coldiron
Second Edition © 2025 Nightswan Press & St. Rooster Books

ALSO BY THE AUTHOR

GOOD BOY
BELLA'S BOYS
THE DEATH LIST
THE GOD PROVIDES
A PRAYER FROM THE DEAD
IMMORAL DILEMMAS
WE ARE 13

COMING SOON

WHIRLWIND
THE CURSE OF KATIE ELDER
THE WITCH OF NOVEMBER
THE TELLING OF THE BEES

SUMMERHOME
THOMAS R CLARK

ST. ROOSTER BOOKS
ONEIDA, NY

PRAISE FOR SUMMERHOME

"If your greatest fears involve aging, infirmity, senile dementia, and a miserable, lonely, humiliating decline, then SummerHome is the book for you, because things could still get so, so much worse!" - *Christine Morgan, author of Lakehouse Infernal and Trench Mouth*

"An unconventional mélange that comes together into something wild and challenging. Exemplary splatstick" - *Garrett Cook, author of Charcoal*

"In his stunning debut novel, Thomas R Clark weaves an original story. Skillfully told, all that resides and remains in Summerhome is sure to haunt you." - *Ruthann Jagge, author of The New Girls' Patient*

"Not since Lansdale's Bubba Ho Tep has a setting like this been used so perfectly. Clark knocks SummerHome one out of the park with a blend of folk lore and modern horror." - *Robert Ford, author of Burner*

"A poignant and graphic tale, a combination of folklore and splatterpunk that grabs you by both the mind and guts and twists them together into balloon animals that will sit in the shadows of your thoughts for days." - *Lisa Lee Tone - Bibliophilia Templum*

"Summer is the time for relaxation, family, sun, and fun. SummerHome has family… and old people sex, an evil ass cat, as well as butt tentacles. Clark forces us to read his nightmares and live vicariously through them. You will not be prepared for how dark and brutal this novel gets." - *Christina Pfieffer MOTHERS OF MAYHEM Podcast*

"Thomas R Clark has crafted an incredible and immersive tale full of terror, ancient lore, and undeniable family ties in Summerhome, where more than blood binds these residents together." - *Candace Nola, author of BISHOP*

"A real, smooth, easy read that was riveting and very addictive!" – *Corrina Morse, No Remorse Reviews*

"Masterfully blending the aesthetics of 'The Visit', 'The Taking of Deborah Logan' with Paul Tremblay's 'Head Full of Ghosts' and Adam Nevill's 'The Reddening' and 'Cunning Folk' sprinkled brilliantly with some Mark Towse humor and geriatric horrors; This is an altogether unique beast on its own." – *Pan Book Reviews & Reccomendations*

In memory of a son named **Joshua**, a friend named **Troy**, a father named **Tyler**, a mother & daughter named **Suzy**, and a son named **Josh**. It's a cycle only we can break...

TABLE OF CONTENTS

ALSO BY THE AUTHOR 4

PART ONE: HAUNTED HOUSES.....................13

CHAPTER 1: The Ghosts of Their Mothers........15

CHAPTER 2: The Haunted Warehouse 25

CHAPTER 3: Tour of Duty 39

CHAPTER 4: Outbursts of Endearment.............51

CHAPTER 5: Karaoke Night 63

CHAPTER 6: Dreams Come True.......................76

CHAPTER 7: Fencing 89

CHAPTER 8: Butterflies 97

CHAPTER 9: Shit Ball...102

CHAPTER 10: Just Another Day.........................115

CHAPTER 11: Dark Memories 129

CHAPTER 12: Milk Cartons..................................137

PART TWO: THE PARAHUNTERS 147

CHAPTER 13: The Trial of Isle Magee................149

CHAPTER 14: Omens 158

CHAPTER 15: Viral...168

CHAPTER 16: Media Circus..................................183

CHAPTER 17: Personal Darkness........................189

CHAPTER 18: My Precious 201

CHAPTER 19: Never Trust a Witch 212

CHAPTER 20: College Days.................................218

CHAPTER 21: Sacrifices..224

CHAPTER 22: Sex and Magic............................228

CHAPTER 23: The Transference......................236

CHAPTER 24: Wet Dreams 239

PART THREE: WITCHWOOD & IRON..........247

CHAPTER 25: Old Gods Never Die 249

CHAPTER 26: Waking the Dead 255

CHAPTER 27: Fire and Rain 269

CHAPTER 28: Special Deliveries 286

CHAPTER 29: Blood is Coming 296

CHAPTER 30: Mistaken Identities.....................313

CHAPTER 31: Reaped.....................................325

CHAPTER 32: ...and Sewn 338

ACKNOWLEDGEMENTS.................................341

ABOUT THE AUTHOR 343

Also Available from St Rooster Books............344

Part One

Haunted Houses

CHAPTER 1: The Ghosts of Their Mothers

A week after her kids moved Maureen Coleman into SummerHome assisted living community, she saw the ghost of her first husband. The wretched stench of the dead woke her up at two in the morning, and she found John standing at the foot of her bed, pointing, taunting her. Though he'd haunted her for a perceived eternity, Maureen couldn't recall another point where she'd seen his spirit manifest.

It terrified a portion of her, a part deep within her mind, where all of her *knew what this manifestation heralded.* John's incorporeal visage mouthed words she could not hear. But somehow, she could feel them, and they turned the tips of her fingers numb with cold.

Thy time is nigh! Maureen felt the words and they made her shiver and weep. She knew the departed spoke the truth.

This! Ye did this! Over and over, and over again! John's spirit shamed her, a dark slit in his throat fluttered as his ethereal lips moved.

"Yes! Yes, we, we did! It is all our fault!" Maureen cried out, "Sean and Meghan, none of the kids, they've never believed a word we've said. But it's all true! All of it! We were a horrible mother and a horrible wife! We're everything they say about us! We should have paid for our sins so long ago!"

A horrible person, it said with inaudible words, *an evil person, possessed to be the concubine of the Divil's spawn!* John's ghost's mouth opened wider than his mortal jaw ever would. It transformed into a gaping maw, housing a swirling vortex of negative energy. Maureen stared at it, transfixed on John's supernatural form. Mourning long overdue filled her with grief her body ached to purge. Maureen couldn't deny this accusation, and its truth shook her to the blackened core of her soul. She wept and wailed. Tears poured down her cheeks.

A loud knocking on Maureen's door broke her catatonia. She pulled her blanket up to her mouth and chewed on the edge. *Who would be trying to come into her house at this time of night?* And then Maureen remembered, she lived in SummerHome, now. She wasn't at her family's home anymore. Her kids saw to her relocation. To them, it's just a house where they live.

But it's so much more.

"Maureen? It's Charmane, the overnight nurse. Are

you decent? I'm coming in." Maureen heard keys jingle and the tumblers of a lock falling. The door opened up, the lights flicked on, and John's ghost disappeared. "Maureen, are you okay? I heard you shouting at someone when I walked by."

Charmane, who possessed a permanent smile and a penchant for wearing brightly colored scrubs honoring her Caribbean ancestry, walked into Maureen's bedroom to find her clenching a blanket, terror covering her face. A rank, sickly sweet odor filled the room. It reminded Charmane of the smell of a dead body. She'd found more than her share of them in this profession. Thankfully Maureen still lived.

"Pew, did someone have an accident? Maureen?" The nurse lost her breath for a moment. Not from Maureen, who lay in bed, her eyes agape. Instead, something Charmane didn't expect sent a shiver up her spine. A pair of yellow, glowing orbs, floating in the air above her patient, flashed at her from the darkness.

"*Dous Jezi!*" Charmane said in Haitian and made the sign of the cross. She often slipped into her native tongue when stressed. Having the shit scared out of you also helped. Her heart pounded against her rib cage as fear triggered her thyroid to release defensive hormones throughout her body.

Then she saw the mundane source of the floating

eyes and laughed at her reaction. Curled up into a ball at the bottom of the bed, peeking at the nurse, was a chonker of a tabby cat, big and gray with a brilliant white diamond on its chest. Its eyes reflected the light from the other room. Charmane allowed an animal to scare her. She breathed a sigh of relief. The cat disappeared into the darkness. The nurse felt her heart rate slow.

"Hello, Maureen, what's wrong? Did you mess yourself?" Charmane asked her patient.

"No, I did not mess myself! I swear by all that's holy my husband is standing at the end of my bed staring at me," Maureen said, speaking in a trembling whisper. Charmane looked around. The lingering smell dissipated, much to her joy.

"No one's here but us, Maureen. If that was a fart, I'd go poop. It means you have to poop when it smells that bad."

"I do not have to poop! He's not here now! The lights are on!"

"Is that so?" Charmane asked.

"Yes."

"You know ghosts aren't real, right?"

"Says who?"

"Says every scientist and me, now check this out."

"What are you-" Maureen lost her words.

Without any indication, Charmane switched off the

light. Darkness and shadow enveloped the room.

"See any ghosts?"

Maureen did, but she couldn't tell the nurse. Instead, she shook her head.

In the gray twilight near where Charmane stood, John re-emerged from the shadows. In his ethereal hand, he held a long, black rapier, etched with inverted crosses and demonic sigils. Maureen shook in fear, unable to speak any intelligible words. Instead of affirmation, what came out of her lips resembled pidgin gibberish.

Charmane didn't see him, *but she could smell ...something*. The horrible odor returned, *if only for a moment*.

"See, Maureen? I don't see any ghosts and if I don't see any ghosts, you know what that means?" Charmane patted the bed. The gray tabby whose markings blended in with the shadows, slinked off the bed as cats will do. Maureen didn't care. Her focus was behind Charmane.

"Did you let out another silent one?" Charmane wrinkled her nose, "Woman, you need to go. Really."

"He's right next to you..." Maureen whispered, managing somehow to put the words together.

"There's no one in here but you and me, Maureen." John's spirit raised the sword and drove it at Charmane's head. Maureen's eyes grew in awe, and a mournful wail erupted from her mouth.

"No!" Maureen screeched as the nurse flicked the light switch back on.

John's murderous revenant flickered away before the sword's blade connected. Maureen's mouth fell agape, filling with saliva until it overfilled, and drool leaked down her chin, soaking her nightgown.

"Oh no, let me clean you up, lady, you're sure you don't have to poop?" Charmane said and Maureen shook her head. The nurse wiped the mess on the old woman's chin clean with a fresh paper napkin, "Maureen, honey, it's okay, there's nothing here. That's all I was showing you. There's no such thing as ghosts. You'll be happy to know there ain't no bigfoot, either. That's just some crazy lumberjacks wanting to scare away hippies. I saw that on the History Channel one day."

"But he tried to kill you." Maureen's words shook as she spoke.

"Why would the ghost of your husband want to kill me?" Charmane asked.

"Because you're taking care of me. He wants us to suffer."

"That's silly."

"We told Sean and Meghan this would happen! I told them not to bring us here!"

"No, no. They did the right thing. We're here to take

care of you when they can't. Here, take this." Charmane offered Maureen a small cup of water and a pill. "This will help you sleep for the rest of the night. Wouldn't you like that?"

"Yes. That would be nice." Maureen conceded. She took the pill and gulped down the water, taking the sleep aid with it.

"There you go, lady. I'm going to go now. If you need me for anything, you can just hit the alarm on the side of your bed, okay?"

"Okay, thank you."

"You're welcome, Mrs. Coleman. Goodnight."

Maureen watched as Charmane turned off the bedroom light and left. The cat followed her into the living room, drifting in and out of the shadows as it padded along.

Of course, John's ghost reappeared instantly, too, still wielding the black sword. But instead of tormenting Maureen, it followed the nurse. Maureen watched John's spirit shimmer and rush at the nurse, the sword brandished high above his head.

Once Charmane, the cat now at her heel, reached the apartment door and turned off the light next to it, she stopped as she turned the knob.

"Goodnight again, Mrs. Coleman," Charmane said.

John's ghost wasted no time in striking. He brought

the sword blade down faster than last time, as she opened the door. The light from the hall burst in, catching the revenant in its glow and disintegrating it. He missed, again.

The cat, however, took the opportunity to rub up against her leg as Charmane stepped out, and disappeared into the light. The nurse hesitated, reached down, and rubbed her ankle before moving along. The door closed behind her and darkness returned to the apartment.

Maureen watched John's spirit return to her room. He taunted her more, it's all he could do. She knew its goal, to torment her much like Marley did Scrooge in A Christmas Carol. But there would be no ghosts of Christmas Past, Present, or Future to force Maureen Coleman to repent for her sins on this night.

The pill Charmane gave her had other plans, and none of which required John's specter. It disregarded his ethereal hazing. The pill didn't care about ghosts, guilt, or regret. No, instead it preferred to clench what remained of her mind in a vice grip and drag her back to sleep.

•

Charmane took the bus home the following morning when her shift ended, more tired than usual. Her ankle ached something fierce. She assumed she twisted it, or sat funny at some point on the ride home. Though this was a Monday morning, it was Charmane's Friday, or better yet her weekend, the beginning of two days off in succession. The last thing she wanted was to have trouble walking.

When she got home, her whole body ached. The woman went straight to bed, and spent the next day in her pajamas, pissed off she caught a summer bug. Her sense of smell was all off. Nothing smelled good to her, everything reeked of decay.

It would be two more days before anyone checked in on Charmane after a no-call, no-show at SummerHome. A concerned relative went to her trailer in Casual Estates, three days later, after a horrible storm caused a blackout and no one heard from her.

By then she was dead, and the fires of Hell, if one believed in such Christian notions, spread through SummerHome and burned it to the ground.

CHAPTER 2: The Haunted Warehouse

Sean Spencer wiped the sweaty strands of hair off his forehead and stepped into the service elevator at Donahue's Furniture warehouse. He pulled the stringy black mess back and tied it off in a ponytail. The tip hung into the middle of his back.

With his hair secured, he jammed the elevator into gear. Someplace on the sixth floor of the building, a reclining chair awaited him. He engaged the elevator's mechanism, pulled the door closed, and up it went. He tapped his fingers on the wood as the car rose.

The control arm, a gnarled, varnished knotty stub, fit perfectly into the palm of a person's hand. It was rumored to be the walking stick of Mr. Donahue, or the shillelagh of Mr. Fitzgerald, depending on who told the story. Regardless of who walked with it, someone long ago attached it to the machine and there it remained, ever since.

The sick-sweet stench of the elevator shaft crept up through the crack between the elevator and the floor. The nausea cocktail included rotting garbage, decaying small animals, grease, oil, and dust. It made Sean's nose wrinkle.

You never get used to the smell, he thought to himself. After two years working at the warehouse in downtown Fenton, New York, the stench of the shaft became synonymous with his daily grind.

The seven-story building featured a unique facade covering the top of the elevator shaft. Resembling a red farmhouse, it stood out as the most recognizable feature of the Fenton skyline. Over the years, it grew to become a thing of legend in the surrounding communities.

Some said the eccentric Mr. Donahue or his former partner, Mr. Fitzgerald-again, depending on who told the story- lived in the 'house.' Now, decades later, *their* benevolent spirits haunted it, keeping watchful eyes on the company he helped build.

The warehouse crew could neither confirm nor deny any of these rumors when they took the elevator to any of the floors, or for breaks in the facade, where they always smoked a joint or two. The warehouse furniture handlers dubbed it 'The Haunted Mansion.'

Sean looked forward to his two o'clock break when

his time came and he could sneak off and catch a buzz. Working in a furniture warehouse got boring, and a little pick me up during the day helped make it go by faster with less tedium. Unfortunately, sometimes this led to errant loaves of bread, or worse, being sewn into the arms of sofas.

The sixth floor came quickly, and Sean released his grip on the device. The car stopped moving. He pulled the door open to reveal a large room lined with large cardboard boxes. Bins rose twelve feet into the air, with three levels, each filled with boxes of reclining chairs. Sean looked at the SKU of the piece he needed on the paper in his hand. He knew where it might be. He put it there earlier in the week. He grabbed a two-wheeled hand cart and made his way to the chair.

Overhead, a screeching whine erupted, a signal someone in the office depressed the *Talk* button on the warehouse intercom.

"Spence," Gorman, the warehouse manager, said, addressing Sean by his last name. Nobody called anyone by their first name in the warehouse, "you up there?" He didn't wait for Sean to respond to the intercom talk-box, "When you come down, you've got a phone call. It's your sister. Something about your mother." The squelch created an ear-piercing amount of feedback as Gorman turned it off.

Great, Sean thought, *of course! It has to be Mom.* Meghan never called unless it involved Mom. Why this couldn't wait until after work, he didn't know. The company's policy forbade cell phones in the warehouse during company time. She knew this. Yet she always called him at work, right after lunch. She'd want him to leave work early to do something with Mom. He'd tell her he can't, this is why we moved her to SummerHome. He'd then tell her he would go see Mom after work at three-thirty, and he hoped to see Meghan there, too. She'd resign and say she'd leave work early then.

He picked up the pace and located the reclining chair. *Wonderful,* his internal monologue continued. The packaged chair sat at the bottom of a stack, four boxes high. He assessed the situation, and the Jenga engineer in his head came up with a plan of retrieval.

He shifted the three boxes on top to the left. The stack moved about four inches and came to rest on the edge of the neighboring bottom box. He then wiggled the bottom box out from under the others. When it came out far enough, he bridged the gap by moving the bottom box on the right underneath. Sean kicked the two-wheeler under the chair he needed and pulled it the rest of the way out into the aisle, and swung it back around in the direction he wanted to take it.

Sean didn't see the tower of chair boxes tip as he

walked by. The squeak of the wheels hid the sound of ripping cardboard as one of the support boxes collapsed. He did feel the change in air pressure as the boxes tumbled. The top of the stack fell into an empty bay across the aisle. The second and third got hung up on the boxes next to them. They hung across the aisle in a widow's peak.

"Fuck!" Sean shouted as he dropped his grip on the two-wheeler. His cargo slapped onto the aisle as he slid alongside it. He could have been squished. He leaned up against the chair, catching his breath. "Thank you, Mr. Donahue or Mr. Fitzgerald. Whichever one of you saved me," he said to the legendary spirits of the warehouse, "we'll smoke one later."

Once his heartbeat slowed down, he got back to work and carted the chair back to the elevator. He closed the door and drove the car back down the shaft to the first floor. The stink of the shaft returned and grew in intensity the closer he got to the bottom. He hit the first floor, sprung the door open, and pulled the chair out. Meghan could wait for him to drop the chair off in the finishing shop, next to Gorman's office. Something smelled good, overpowering the elevator shaft's stench. Though Sean ate lunch an hour before, it made his mouth water.

He pulled the chair into the shop next to a man

working on a large headboard. Miz, the shop foreman, gave Sean the 'man nod' as he walked in. Miz's real last name was Mizouni, his parents immigrated to the States from Iraq long before the wars. When he spoke his surname, he rolled his r's.

Miz skillfully manipulated a marker to cover a blemish on the headboard. The rest of the bed was scattered about the shop. Sean noted the triskelion spiral pattern indicating this was a Brannigan Farms piece. Next to Stickley and Harden, Brannigan Farms made the most expensive furniture Donahue's sold.

"Hey, Miz," Sean said and parked the two-wheeler in an open space on the floor.

"Hey, Spence," Miz twisted the end of his thin mustache like a movie villain when he talked to people, "watch your cart, this is the new Mountain Ash line I'm working on. Super expensive shit and I don't want to fix a nick."

"Oh, don't worry. I'm well aware. I remember unloading it when it came in. Why they want it stored on the Seventh Floor is beyond me."

"It's so nothing else might damage it. Nothing else there but carpeting."

"That's another thing that's always puzzled me," Sean knew carpeting rolls weighed a ton, and always required a tow motor to move. The seventh floor had a dedicated tow motor for carpet.

"What's that delicious smell?"

"My wife made me sabich. For lunch."

"Again? The last time she made you sabich, Wayne lost the pita you gave him in the arm of the recliner he was working on. You weren't there three weeks later when we went to the lady's house. The fucking eggs smelled nice and rancid."

"Like a dead body. Hah, no, this I kept it all for myself," he laughed, "what you smell, lingering in the air, is all that's left." He patted his belly.

"Here's the chair you needed."

"Thanks. That's it?" He pointed to the box. Sean nodded in affirmation, "Perfect spot to leave it. I can take it out of the box. You going on break at two?"

"Sure am. On the way up we need to stop on six and restack a couple of chairs that fell over. The ghost was looking out for me, man, deflected that shit. It almost fell on top of me."

"Damn!" Miz replied, an expression of awe on his face.

"Okay, I gotta run, my sister is waiting for me on the phone. We'll see you up in the Mansion later."

"That you will! Peace," Miz replied as Sean left the finishing shop.

Meghan Coleman closed the call on her phone, a blank expression covering her face. Dr. Al-Mahairi from SummerHome called and indicated his concern for her mother. Her condition was deteriorating and he was questioning their decision to place her at SummerHome and not a full care nursing facility.

Maybe Covid and the pandemic were a factor? She kept the thought to herself.

He requested a meeting with Meghan and her brother, Sean, as soon as possible. She explained to him they would be there tonight, as they are every night, visiting their mother. A meeting with the doctor wasn't out of the question.

She went to the sink and filled a glass up through the tap, swirled the water about, dumped it, then refilled it. It was a habit she had taken up growing up on a lake with well water. Other than smelling of sulfur and tasting like liquid farts, well water would bring sediment up from the earth, and the first glass full was always dirty and full of floating bits of sediment. She didn't need to do it anymore, not since the city put real water pipes in a few years ago, but the habits of youth are hard to break. She took a long refreshing drought of the grit-free, city water and sighed.

She stared at her phone a moment longer, her home screen a candid family selfie featuring Meghan along with her brother and their Mom. Everyone is smiling. Mom looks so healthy and vibrant. The picture might be five years old?

I can't believe how far downhill she's gone, she thought, *ever since her stroke, and so fast,* she thought as she dialed her brother. Meg knew he would be at work.

She didn't care.

This was about Mom and she would call him. Why he didn't bring his cell phone to work bothered her. Especially with Mom being at the assisted-living home. She didn't care if the company's policy forbade cell phones in the warehouse. She knew he brought it with him the last time he got a girlfriend, but he couldn't bring it with him for Mom.

The lack of sleep didn't help. Meghan and Sean both slept, as she did most nights, in the family's house in their respective bedrooms. If she could sleep at all. Ever since her mother's condition started making itself known, the stress of caring for her brought on nightmares for the young woman.

The dreams themselves were never, how could she put it, scary? It's the content of the dreams, what they were, and this scared her the most. Last night was no different. It lingered with her.

A dozen claps of thunder rolled and showers fell from on high, consecrating the ground and all within. Meghan stood, her eyes closed with her arms outstretched, doused in the blessed water.

She could smell the salty air, and feel the moisture covering her naked body. She opened her eyes, to discover the rain was crimson.

The rain fell and blessed all it touched.

"Donahue's warehouse, this is Chris, how can I help you?" Her brother's supervisor's voice broke her from her memory.

"Hi, Chris. Sean Spencer, please."

"Who's calling?"

"It's Meghan and it's an emergency. Something with our mother."

"Of course, it is. Hold the line, please."

Meghan watched the minutes tick by on her phone while she waited for her brother. Fifteen cold, thoughtless minutes passed before she heard her brother's voice come out of the phone's speaker.

"Meghan? You there?" Sean said. Her green eyes lit up when he spoke.

"It's about time," she looked at the phone timer, "it's been fifteen minutes."

"I'm at work, Meghan. What's up? You want me to get my dead ends cut again?"

"Hah hah, very funny big brother. I know you won't leave work early, but can you meet me at Mom's when you get out today?" She twisted her curly auburn hair with a free finger.

"Sure can, I go there every night, you do, too."

"I know we do, I'm there with you, Sean," she mimicked him speaking, squinching her features and crossing her eyes.

"I know you are. Why are you talking in circles and why the call?"

"Apparently Mom had an incident last night."

"An incident? What happened? Did she get out?"

"No, no. Nothing like that. She said Dad's ghost was in her bedroom."

"Oh shit, that's not good," she heard her brother sigh in despair. "Which Dad? My dad or your dad?"

"I don't know. Have you ever been able to get out of her who your father was?"

"No. But I overheard her saying once his name was Dave and he was a photographer."

"She had so many secrets."

"I know. What did you call about, Meghan?"

"So, we need to talk to the doctor about maybe having her meds looked at if she's hallucinating."

"Good idea," Sean said.

"Okay, that's it. I'll see you this afternoon. Love you," she said.

•

"Love you, too," Sean said, waited for his sister to hang up, and placed the office phone's receiver back in its cradle. The warehouse still used a rotary dial phone. Some younger employees didn't know how to use it.

"I've been meaning to ask you this, Spence," Gorman said. Chris Gorman stood five foot nothing and could kick the tar out of a one-way street's blacktop. He sported a military brush cut, a pierced eyebrow, and always wore wrap-around shades-hiked up his forehead when inside. He also possessed a sarcastic sense of humor the handlers in the warehouse respected.

"What's that?" Sean asked.

"You and your step-sister there got some Only Fans thing going on I don't know about?" Gorman managed to say before bursting into laughter.

"Very funny. She's my sister, well, half my biological sister, not my step-sister. We have the same mother, different fathers. So, no," Sean replied.

"Uh-huh. I don't think I believe you. But if you say nothing's going on, then," Gorman winked at Sean, who rolled his eyes and shook his head in disapproval,

"And don't you get any ideas," Sean added, "she's saving herself for her husband. It's a promise she made to our mother."

"That's a shame. She does have two other-" Sean coughed loudly, masking Gorman's crude comment.

"She's my sister, remember?"

"You've got no sense of humor. Whatcha got going on now?"

"I gotta go back up to six and fix a stack of chairs then I'm taking my break."

"Great. Sucks about your Mom, I kinda know what yer going through, I experienced it with my Nana. My aunts and uncles all fighting and shit over her stuff after they put her in the home. It's good to see you and your sister getting along with this going on."

"She can be a pain in the ass sometimes," Sean said.

"That's what I want to hear, I thought her name was Meg, not Peg," Gorman raised the pierced eyebrow and smirked. He thrust his pelvis forward.

"Dude. Really?" Sean laughed, he knew Gorman wasn't serious, but he played along and pretended to be angry, "She's my little sister. She's ten years younger than me, you know this right?"

"Hah hah!" Gorman guffawed, in typical fashion, he changed the subject. "I'll see ya up in the Haunted Mansion later!"

Sean shook his head, smiled, and left the office. He returned to the elevator and its stench, thinking about his Mom and ghosts.

"Ghosts are everywhere, ha?" He said to no one in particular and pulled the door closed.

CHAPTER 3: Tour of Duty

Sean and Meghan sat in Doctor Al-Mahairi's office, waiting for him to retrieve the nurse's report from the night before. Silence floated in the air between the brother and sister, not wanting to talk about their mother's more frequent hallucinations and what they implied. Instead, the siblings stared at the walls, covered with Dr. Al-Mahairi's degrees in fancy frames.

A stack of pamphlets for SummerHome stood on a display on an end table. Sean grabbed one and read the back. A beautiful photograph of the property graced the top third of the paper.

SummerHome by Forward Frontiers Inc., or FFI, is an assisted living community in Fenton, NY. With twenty-five private, luxurious two-bedroom apartments, and respected staff of doctors, nurses, custodians, and CNAs,

SummerHome's residents live normal lives under limited supervision. Each resident's health needs are addressed by a medical staff present twenty-four hours a day, seven days a week.

At SummerHome, we know the secret to a long life is exercising the mind as well as the body. Daily activities, including everything from yoga to karaoke, power walking, and who can forget everyone's favorite: BINGO! Three scheduled meals and encouraged interaction with their peers give our residents the daily structure they desire. But it's the freedom for our residents to do as they please that makes the SummerHome community something more than a nursing home. All of this makes it a house! And dare we say it's your house?

SummerHome. Making Old Age Liberating.

Sean shook his head and returned the flier to the stack. He questioned himself and the decision to move Mom into SummerHome in the first place. Taking care of her after her stroke was a full-time job neither Sean nor Meghan could fulfill.

Did they do the right thing, bringing Mom here?

If he vocalized this thought, Meghan would remind him how six months later they found Mom limping down Route 104 in her PJs at midnight, during a rainstorm. The doubt continued to nag at Sean. He shifted and squirmed in his seat until the door opened and Dr. Al-

Mahairi entered his office with a thick manila folder, full of papers.

"Sorry about this," he read Charmane's report recounting the multiple, waking nightmares. Sean and Meghan grew more melancholy as he went into the details, "It's possible your mother's dementia is becoming early-onset Alzheimer's, yes. But we can't be sure without some further testing, and that's going to require another MRI, which she doesn't respond well to if you recall."

"No. She freaks the fuck out inside them is what she does," Sean Spencer, Maureen Coleman's older child replied.

"That she does," Meghan Coleman, his younger sister, concurred.

"There's what, eleven years between the two of you?"

"Yeah. Why do you ask?" Sean asked the doctor.

"It's good to see children so involved with their mother. She had you both late in life?"

"Yes. She was forty-five when I was born," Meghan revealed, "she promised my dad a little girl, and he got it. Now he's dead and I'm about to be a twenty-one-year-old woman in less than a month."

"And a pain," he winked at his sister, "Thanks for acknowledging that, Doc, we appreciate it," Sean said. Meghan slapped him on the back of the head.

"I'll give you a pain with my foot. Wiseass," Meghan poked back at her brother's comments, "and yes, thank you Doctor Al-Mahairi. That was kind of you to say."

"It's my pleasure. I wish more of our resident's children were like you two."

"We're just normal people trying to cope," Sean added.

"I can see that. We can suggest counseling for you both if you like. It could help you understand this process more. We also have a group meeting once a week for the loved ones of those suffering from personality changes in dementia and Alzheimer's patients."

"I think we'd like to know more about the group, at the very least, since we come here so often already," Meghan said.

"Very good, the next meeting is next week, Thursday at eight-thirty, do you think you could make it? We call that past their bedtime here. I'll pencil both of you in so we can have enough chairs?"

"It's a little short notice, but sure," Meghan answered, "Sean, what about you?" She asked her brother.

"Um, yeah, I can do that." Sean agreed, "how long does it last?"

"Just an hour," Dr. Al-Mahairi said, "We all talk it out, give each other advice on how to cope. Now, as far as your mother is concerned, I'll be setting her up for tests this week during the day. If anything comes up, who should I call first?"

"Call me," Meghan raised her hand and volunteered, "Sean can't take calls at his work." Sean looked at his sister and furrowed his brow.

Did she really just say that? Miss Telephone Switchboard Operator? When she didn't catch his stare down, Sean shook his head as if to say *'Are you fucking kidding me?'* She shrugged her shoulders, oblivious, it seemed, to how she pulled her brother's trigger.

"Yeah, I'm hard to reach. Calling Megs is best." He rolled his eyes and crossed his arms, shaking his head again.

"Very good, so we will go visit your mother now and see how she is doing."

"We'd love to. Thank you Dr. Al-Mahairi," Sean stood and shook the man's hand.

"Yes, thank you," added Meghan.

"You are most welcome. It's my pleasure. This way, please," and Dr. Al-Mahairi led them to the door.

•

SummerHome bustled with activity. The elderly shuffled about, going to wherever they may be going, with or without the aid of walkers, wheelchairs, or canes. The nursing staff went about with their med carts, knocking on apartment doors. Sean and Meghan followed Dr. Al-Mahairi as the physician weaved between staff, guests, and residents until a grizzled custodian pushing a mop bucket stopped the doctor. He feathered his short, but thick, mop of salt and pepper hair. The toes of beat-up cowboy boots, held together with duct tape, stuck out from under the legs of his yellow custodial overalls.

"Hey Doc," his words lisped and the man's lips curled into his toothless mouth as he spoke, "can you check on Mrs. Webster? She's been complaining about wanting to throw up for three days now. Keeps saying something smells bad in the hallway. I checked and there's nothing I can smell. She's ninety years old, maybe her sniffer is busted?"

"Thank you, RJ. I doubt her sniffer is busted. Did you say anything to her nurse?" The Doctor questioned.

"No, no I haven't," RJ replied, he turned his head down and shook it. His name badge declared him to be one RICHARD JAMES. Sean noted the orderly possessed two first names, making him more of a stereotype for a north country redneck.

"That's okay, RJ, you didn't do anything wrong. Let her know what you told me; can you do that?" The janitor nodded and pushed his bucket down the hall away from them. The doctor waited until the man was out of earshot, "He takes care of one of the residents, Marion Webster. Her granddaughter disappeared twenty-five or so years ago, and the girl was engaged to RJ. So, they're pretty close, it's as if he's family. We encourage our staff who know our residents to engage with them thus."

"Oh, RJ, I need to speak with you. And hi, Doc!" A diminutive, silver-haired woman dressed in black said. She held hands with a bald, mustachioed man almost twice her height. He was a NASCAR fan, declaring his allegiance to the memory of the late Dale Sr. on a T-shirt and ball cap. A big silver necklace declaring her name as *BABS* hung around her neck, shining in the fluorescent lights.

"Hello, Babs," the doctor replied, then acknowledged her partner, "hello, Bill." Bill nodded back, acknowledging the doctor.

"Hey, Babs," RJ interjected. A giant grin covered the woman's face.

"We're going to karaoke tonight in the rec center with the Brooks, VIP Dave and Carry, are you going to join us this week?"

"I'm with a resident's family, as you can see," Dr. Al-Mahairi motioned to Sean and Meghan, "so I won't be coming this week, I'm sorry," the doctor and the siblings moved down the hallway, as the conversation behind them continued.

"I'll be coming down with Marion, Babs," RJ said.

"That's great," the little old lady shouted back. She said something after, but Sean couldn't make it out. He didn't care, he wanted to see his mother and gave zero shits about karaoke.

Then something took him aback, and he felt selfish. A wrinkled man sat alone, facing a chess set. He wore a long tweed jacket, with a tartan scarf wrapped around his neck. This struck Sean as odd for the middle of summer. The old man's eyes were white and lifeless, but his face was deep in thought. A cloudy haze hung about the man, making Sean squint.

He carries a fog around with the coat? Sean pondered as his eyes focused and the blurriness disappeared. Then he made another conclusion: *For a blind man to play chess by himself must be the ultimate act of loneliness.* But Sean quickly realized this wasn't the case. The old man was far from alone at SummerHome.

"Hey Doc, it's your turn," the old man said.

"Ah, I see it is," Doctor Al-Mahairi answered the man, gazing at the chess board, "you moved your Bishop and put my Knight in peril. That's a tough spot to be in."

"Klaus saw it coming."

"Hah, I bet he did. I'll take my turn tonight, Walt, when I have time to think."

"You mean during karaoke?" The old fellow snickered as he spoke.

"Yes, I mean during karaoke."

"You do what you can, but you're still going to lose to an old blind man, kid," the two guffawed, and Sean and Meghan found themselves laughing along in tandem.

"Walt here is a WWII vet and a war hero. He's 99 years old and still gets around, only needs a little help."

"That's right, I'm 97, don't prematurely age me. I joined the Army when I was 14, lied on my application, and said I was my older brother who died from polio. I fought on D-Day."

"Yes, Walt is a war hero, purple heart and all," the doctor added.

"Ain't that the truth. I've got the metal plate in my head and the nuts and bolts in my hip as reminders. You be good now, you hear," Walt said and waved them by, never turning from the game he couldn't see.

They all laughed together and the trio continued on their way.

"Why is he wearing that jacket in July?" Sean asked

the doctor.

"If you ask him, the jacket and scarf are a spoil of war," Dr. Al-Mahairi replied.

"A spoil of war?" Sean's eyebrow raised, inquisitively.

"Yes, he wears the coat and scarf all year long. I've heard the story enough times. Apparently, he took both the scarf and the jacket off an SS officer he shot in Germany. He ran into a squad of stormtroopers in an alley. He shot their commander in the head, and the rest of them ran when they saw Walt's back up behind him. He says he took the coat and scarf because they were manufactured here, in Fenton."

"That's weird," Meghan added. Sean nodded.

"It gets weirder. You heard him mention someone named Klaus?" The siblings nodded in unison, "allegedly that's the ghost of the Nazi he shot. He claims Klaus guides his hand in chess."

"Now that's just plain crazy," Sean said.

"That's just how some people are, no? I'm certain the story is both true and a tall tale. It's these little quirks I find most interesting about the residents here. I'm sure you both have some of your own," Dr. Al-Mahairi raised the question. The siblings couldn't argue this.

They were almost to Maureen's apartment when yet another aged couple cut across their path. This pair moved along at a snail's pace, smiling as they shuffled along.

I'm getting Sunday drivers in a fucking hallway! Sean wondered if they'd ever get to their mother's apartment.

"Good evening Doc!" The portly white-haired man interjected. He held hands with a diminutive blue-haired woman. They appeared to be husband and wife; a fact confirmed by Dr. Al-Mahairi. Sean wondered if they, too, were headed to karaoke.

"Mike, why are you bothering them?" the old lady chastised her husband, "Please forgive my husband. Hey, are you Maureen's kids?"

"Yes, we are." Meghan replied, "I'm Meghan, this is Sean. And who are you?" Sean nodded to the couple.

"I thought so, saw your pictures on her wall. We're Maureen's neighbors, the O'Connors. I'm Gladys, this is Mike. We've been married for almost sixty years; did you know that? November twenty-second, the day that no-good commie shot JFK, is our anniversary!" Sean and Meghan giggled in response, "I'm sorry we're bugging you. It's good to have another nice Irish family in SummerHome. Well, toodles, my king and I have to get back to our apartment for daily shows, don't we?"

"Yes, we do, my dear," an ear-to-ear grin covered Mike O'Connor's face, "Good day!"

"Yes, good day indeed," Gladys said, a mischievous sparkle glimmering in her eye, amplified by her coke-bottle thick glasses. Without another word, the couple shuffled past the siblings. Once they were out of earshot, which meant about a car length away, the doctor shook his head and laughed.

"What is it Doc?" Sean asked.

"Oh, I'm just thinking about Mike and Gladys. They're seventy-eight and eighty-years young. She's legally blind without her glasses. And Mike's Viagra script just arrived."

"You mean?" Meghan's smile turned to a look of disgust.

"Oh yes, I do mean. They're about to get busy, as we used to say."

They watched Mike and Gladys disappear into their apartment. Sean noted they were neighbors, albeit across the hall and kitty-corner, with his mother. A few footsteps later, they reached Maureen's door.

CHAPTER 4: Outbursts of Endearment

The Doctor knocked on the door to apartment thirteen, Maureen Coleman's home for the last few weeks.

"Why are you knocking? It's my mother's apartment, right? I've never had to knock on her door in my life!" Sean declared and opened the door. He stormed in and declared, "Hi, Mom! I brought Meghan and a Doctor with me."

Gray-haired and frail, Maureen sat in her lift chair, watching Judge Judy repeats on TV, and crocheting a blanket. Her wrinkled hands and gnarled fingers moved the thick needles on memory impulse. For a woman in her mid-sixties, she appeared to be decades older, ancient and decrepit. Age spots covered her exposed skin, resembling cancerous freckles. One of the larger liver spots covered the tip of her nose, and thick hairs resembling a patch of cactus thorns grew out of it.

"You're here early today," Maureen put her needlework down.

"Hi, Mom," Meghan kissed her mother on the forehead. The elder Coleman gently patted her daughter's arm and hugged it to her cheek.

"Hello Mrs. Coleman, I'm Doctor Al-Mahairi, how are you today?"

"Hello, doctor. I'm pretty good, same as usual. I don't want to be here; I'd rather be back in my own house. But other than that, I'm fine. Some damn strangers are living in my house now. Probably tearing it to shreds and partying all night."

"The house is all good, Mom." Meghan assured their mother, "no one is living there but me."

"So you say," Maureen smiled, her mouth a picket fence of broken and missing teeth. She needed dental work but refused to see a dentist. Maureen Coleman was many things, and her children knew all too well how obstinance topped the list of her favorite pastimes, "That's nice."

"I heard you had a visitor last night." The doctor asked her.

"Yeah. I sure did. And not just last night, it's been every night since I got here, I think. Just last night I woke up to pee and there he was, standing at the end of my bed," she grabbed Meghan's arm and looked her in the eyes, "my dead husband came here. He was pissed at me. He tried killing the nurse, too. I'm glad he didn't. I like her."

"Who tried killing the nurse?" Doctor Al-Mahairi asked, a look of concern on his face.

"Was it Dad?" Meghan asked.

"Your father is Joe, this was my other husband, John," she replied as if spectral beings were commonplace, "he had this long, wicked sword and..." Maureen stopped talking and stared off, looking at nothing. Her face went blank, her eyes stared without blinking.

"Mom?" Meghan asked, "are you okay?" Maureen didn't answer her daughter. Instead, she drooled and her lower jaw quivered. An awful odor filled the apartment, stinging Meg's eyes. Then Maureen shot her right arm up and clawed the doctor's face. Her fingernails raked across his cheek, and sent the doctor reeling backward. He fell to the floor.

Sean went to the doctor's aid. Dazed, the man sat up. Blood squirted out between the fingers of the hands he held over the wound.

"Feck you, brownie!" Maureen shouted. Each word slipped further into an Irish accent she never used before, at least not in front of the kids. "They're like flies on shit. This fecking town, all sorts of demon whores and fecking fairies everywhere. Feck ye!"

"Mom! That isn't nice!" Meghan corrected her mother's slurs. "And since when are you a leprechaun?" The accent rang a bell of familiarity with Meghan as if she'd heard it before. Her mother's ranting grew in volume and anger.

"A cross on ye, whore! Ye fecking slut! Yer cunt is a dumpster for disease. We can't believe we chose you!" Maureen spit at her daughter. A great big green loogie splashed onto her cheek. It hung out for a second, then dripped off, onto the faux-hardwood flooring.

Grossed out by the spit, Meghan gasped in astonishment. Sean couldn't believe his ears or his eyes. The doctor didn't give a fuck, his face hurt too much from the old lady scratching him.

"Holy shit Mom, what are you doing?" Sean demanded.

"Ye? A needle dick waste of sperm? An accident is what ye are! A constant reminder of all our failures. We should have aborted both of ye when we had the cha-"

Maureen stopped talking mid-word. She returned to staring at the ceiling as if someone or something flipped a switch inside her head.

"What the fuck is going on? I've never seen her this bad." Sean shook his head in disbelief. There were things a mother never says to their child, and she doubled down on both of them.

Meghan, too, stared at their mother in shock. She wanted to scream back at her, to defend her chaste honor, and remind her mother she was saving herself for her husband. But then she remembered the outburst is a symptom of the disease.

"Her condition is degrading. We all know where this outburst came from, we were just discussing it in the hall." The doctor said, his voice muffled from his hands covering his face. Sweat beaded on his forehead. "I'm afraid if the medication doesn't work, we won't be able to care for her, she'll need to go to a full-fledged nursing home and care facility. We can't have the residents assaulting staff or other residents."

Sean and Meghan knew this could be disastrous. Before either could respond, Maureen spoke up without warning.

"Oh my! What happened to you, Doctor?" She acted as if her outburst and the accompanying violence never happened, "what happened to your face, doctor?"

"Oh, nothing. I scratched myself. You know how we doctors can be sometimes." Dr. Al-Muhairi hid his anger at getting clawed. He tried to placate Mrs. Coleman, fearing he might set off another incident. Telling dementia patients about blackouts often resulted in a relapse.

"Oh yes, I do. Now, what were we discussing? I thought we were talking about John trying to kill that lovely nurse last night."

"Who is John, Mom? You said it was your husband, remember? Was it my Dad or Sean's Dad?" Meghan asked, interrupting her mother. *My father's name was Joe. Sean's Dad was a Donny,* she mentally noted, knowing her family's members.

"I know my husband's name. John tried killing her," Maureen rolled her eyes, obviously irritated her daughter spoke up, "Anyway, what's the nurse's name? Charmin? Don't squeeze her? What a cute name. Pretty girl."

"Charmane is her name, Maureen." The Doctor informed her.

"Oh, that's right. Pretty. Really pretty," she coughed and hackled a bit of phlegm up.

"Now if you'll excuse me, I need to tend to this." Dr. Al-Mahairi said.

"Oh yes, please do!" Maureen said.

"We're going to go with him, Mom," Sean told his mother, "he needs our help."

"Okay. Are you coming back?" Maureen's lips frowned, her eyebrows drooped and covered her eyes like a secondary lid of wrinkles.

"Yes, absolutely we're coming back," Meghan assured her mother.

"Then I'll take a little nap until you come back. Judge Judy is boring me today." She turned the television off from its remote and yawned.

"That'll work. We'll see you soon, Mom," Sean told his mother. Meghan kissed her on the forehead, and the trio left, flipping the lights off as they exited.

Nobody noticed the stench of the dead leaving the room, or the gray tabby cat. A white diamond of fur faintly pulsed on its chest as it watched them leave, from the dark of Maureen's bedroom...

•

Sean and Meghan escorted the wounded Doctor back to his office where a nurse could attend to him. He reminded them of the severity of the situation. As embarrassed as the siblings were from the incident, the doctor assured them he would be taken care of. He reinforced his warning, about what would happen if she expressed further violent outbursts.

They left the office together and made their way back to wrap up their daily visit with Mom. The prognosis wasn't good. Their mother attacked the doctor, they felt lucky she didn't hurt a nurse or an aide. If their mother continued to have violent outbursts, she may have to find other accommodations better suited to cater to her needs. And a nursing home would kill her faster than the disease. Not to mention the location would surely be further from Fenton than Sean or Meg would like.

Both siblings wished this day would end. Hunger pangs in their bellies told the brother and sister they needed dinner. The appeal of sitting down with their mother raised their hopes. When they reached Maureen's door, Sean once again failed to knock. He burst right in.

He regretted it by the second step.

"FUCK ME ELVIS!" A woman screamed.

Sean and Meghan both thought their mother might be having an episode. Until they heard a man answer.

"That's right Houston, the King has landed. I repeat, the King has landed!"

Meghan flipped on the light switch by the door.

They didn't expect to see Gladys O'Connor, her eighty-year-old tits sagging a good foot from her chest, bent over her walker. Her wig fell off at some juncture in the lovemaking. It didn't help her cause. Her thinned scalp, bulging eyes, and a gaping toothless mouth made Sean think of Gollum.

It fucks me hard, me precious, it does, oh yes!

The frail old woman, who might have weighed seventy pounds after a trip to an all-you-can-eat buffet, screamed in ecstasy. A large rubber dildo was stuck to a chair in front of her with a suction cup. Gladys opened her toothless maw and licked it before fellating the bulbous tip.

Behind her, dressed in a white jumper with the zipper opened up, stood a grunting Mike O'Connor. His exposed chest, covered in gray hair complimented the black pompadour Elvis wig he wore. He wiggled and thrust with the might of Elvis the Reconstructed Pelvis. Then he smacked Gladys on her bony ass, and a loud crack echoed in the room. Instead, her shriek of pleasure was garbled by the silicone phallus in her mouth. He pushed into his wife so hard the walker moved across the floor and she deep throated the dildo to its base, knocking her forehead on the chair.

"What are you two looking at?" He demanded, "if you came to get your football or frisbee back, I gave them both to my dog, you little bastards, now fuck off, 'cause the King said so!"

"Who are you talking to, Mike?" Gladys said, after removing the dildo from her mouth. Sean realized Mrs. O'Connor didn't have her glasses on. She couldn't see them. Meghan turned off the light, and together with her brother, stepped out of the O'Connors' apartment and shut the door.

"Goddamned paparazzi, baby, that's all. The King took care of them." they heard Mike tell his wife as they exited. The brother and sister stood before the O'Connor's closed door for a few minutes, before breaking out in laughter.

"That's why you knock!" Meghan said, "I can't scrub that vision out of my eyes now. There's not enough bleach in this place to fix that. Thanks."

"Hey, I don't want to hear it, missy. If my memory serves me right, you turned on the motherfucking light," Sean countered, "I hope he didn't break her hip when he spanked her."

"He was really dressed up like Elvis, wasn't he?" Meghan started laughing. Sean followed suit.

•

The siblings took a few steps down the hall, made sure they stood before their mother's apartment and knocked. After what they saw, prudence took precedence.

"It's open!" Maureen Coleman shouted from inside. Sean hoped to God their mother would be dressed. He'd seen more than his fair share of saggy tits for one day. She was.

This visit with Mom ended on a better note. They avoided talking about ghosts, or doctors. There were no outbursts or strange moments where Maureen would stare at nothing. Instead, they ate dinner together, piping hot Stouffer's premade lasagna and Italian bread. They watched Steve Harvey on Family Feud, then Vannah and Pat. And, after the game show hour, they had to watch Para-Hunters, with the Wish dot com version of Ed and Lorraine Warren, The Buffetts, Teddy and Elaine.

Sean wondered if it was a good idea, to let her watch a ghost hunting show after her incident the night before. But she insisted so they watched it. It wasn't long after the show ended when Maureen felt tired and wanted to go to sleep. Sean and Meghan tucked their mom into bed, said goodnight, and within a few minutes, their matriarch was snoring away. The kids waited a few minutes before shutting off the lights and leaving.

·

As soon as the door closed, the tabby cat jumped up on the old woman's bed, kneaded a section at her feet, and curled into a ball.

But Maureen didn't feel it.

After a few minutes, the sleeping cat purred in time with Maureen Coleman's snoring.

But Maureen couldn't hear it...

CHAPTER 5: Karaoke Night

The music of the karaoke show in the rec center could be heard echoing through the halls of the facility. The weekly event was as popular as BINGO, and far more annoying to those residents who didn't participate in the activity. It was hard for Sean and Meghan to ignore when they left their mother's apartment.

Sean swore he heard Elvira, the old Oak Ridge Boys classic. As he and Meghan neared the rec center, and the building's exit, they discovered confirmation of their assumptions.

"Giddy up," Sean said, singing along with the song, "hey, this guy singing is pretty good, he's got that low voice down perfect. I bet he sings in church. I gotta peek in and see who it is."

"No, Sean, don't. You'll see one of the residents we've met and we'll get sucked in. You watch."

"Nope, ain't gonna happen. But I need to know," he pushed the door open.

"Sean, it's getting late, come on," Meghan protested. She grabbed her brother's shoulder, but he ignored her.

"Son of a bitch, this is great, the greatest fucking thing I've seen all day," Sean said as he stood slack jaw in disbelief. RJ, the custodian, sang his heart out. His dance moves were on spot. The janitor clicked the heels of his cowboy boots, country two-stepping in the stage area with his thumbs in his belt. This continued until the song ended.

"That went out to my one true love, Bobbie Be Good, who's been missing almost thirty years, now. I miss you so much, to this day," RJ declared at the end of the song. A collective, gasping "Aw" of empathy came from the attendees, followed by a rising round of applause.

Decorated to resemble a posh nightclub from the Seventies or maybe Eighties, Sean could feel the positive energy in the room. The normally mundane rec center was filled with residents pretending they were any place other than SummerHome. Staff members he recognized as CNAs, LPNs, and RNs were the wait staff and bartenders.

Sean noted Babs and Bill from the hall earlier, making out at their table like teenagers. They sat with another couple, a blonde woman who either invested in wigs or far too much hair dye; and a portly gentleman with a pornstache and giant moobs you could see through his polo shirt. Sean assumed they were the infamous Carry and VIP Dave Brooks.

The karaoke DJ, a man old enough to be a resident wore a shirt declaring his name to be Frankie, affirmed his assumption moments later. He called Carry up to sing an obscure Fleetwood Mac song, one of their later, smaller hits. The matron waddled to the stage. A light shone on her from behind Sean's point of view, filtering through the material of her sun dress. It was evident Carry wasn't wearing a bra. Or panties. Her tits and ass didn't sag, though. Sean was certain VIP Dave and his wallet made sure they stayed perky and wrinkle-free.

Carry took the microphone from Sandy and the song started. In typical karaoke fashion, it wasn't horrible, but it wasn't pleasing to the ear, either.

"It's oldies night, that's for sure," Sean quipped. Meghan jabbed him in the side.

"Sean, that's not right to say here," she shook her head in disapproval.

"What did I say wrong? I mean, did I lie?" He feigned innocence at his borderline inappropriate joke. She crossed her arms and shook her head more.

"Someone might have heard you."

"Over the music? Oh, come on, I swear you're turning

into Mom sometimes, you hit the ripe old age of twenty-one and suddenly we can't have fun anymore? You know what? I think I'm going to sign you up for a karaoke song."

"You will not."

"Watch me," Sean said and made a grand entrance into the faux club, with Meghan in pursuit. He discovered an empty table, next to RJ and a much older woman in a wheelchair. A stack of sign-up slips and a golf pencil, beckoning him on its surface, "well what have we got here?" The pair sat down in the open chairs.

"Sean, this isn't funny."

"I know, Carry's killing my inner ear right now."

"She's not always this bad," RJ leaned over and said, inviting himself into their conversation,

"Is that so?" Meghan answered him.

"Yeah, when she does duets she sings better. If you're here long enough she'll do one with me. Hey, ain't you Maureen's kids? Is she coming?"

"Um, yes we are and no she's not, RJ, right?"

"Yessir, yes ma'am" he smiled. Both Sean and Meghan realized RJ had no teeth.

"But you have the voice of an angel, my dear sister," Sean said and filled out a slip, writing down the name of Meg's favorite song, 'Because the Night' by Natalie Merchant and 10,000 Maniacs, "I hope she has it," he brandished the swatch of paper in his fist. RJ and his elderly companion laughed at Sean's antics.

"Sean! No, I won't do it," she continued to protest and Sean continued to ignore her. He slinked away from the table as Carry's song was ending, and made his way to the DJ "booth," which was nothing more than a card table with a laptop and soundboard.

"Great job on that Fleetwood Mac! Give Carry the clap," the DJ announced on the PA, "we're going to take a brief break, but when we come back, we'll be back at the top of the rotation for the last hour of the show!"

Sean waited while she finished speaking before handing him the slip. Frankie took it from him and reviewed it.

"Is she going to sing?" The DJ asked, "the way she was acting over there tells me she isn't."

"She'll sing," Sean affirmed, doing his best to look her in the eyes.

"Well, you better hope so, because if she doesn't, you will. That's the rules of my karaoke show."

"That's not a problem, thank you. Frankie, is it?" The DJ nodded and Sean went back to the table with his sister.

"I won't sing when he calls my name, you wasted your time," Meghan warned him.

"I guess I'll have to sing it, then."

"What?" Meghan's face wrinkled in disgust, "you'll destroy my favorite song." Sean shrugged his shoulders.

Five minutes later, Sandy fired the karaoke back up.

"We had a late comer in the last round, you guys don't mind if I put her up first, do you?" Frankie asked his faithful crowd of singers. They replied with a round of applause, "Okay then. So, let's get Meghan up here to sing an old Bruce Springsteen song."

Meghan mouthed the word NO over and over to Sean.

"Either you go, or I go, Megs," Sean threatened his sister. He stood.

"Can we have Meghan on the stage, please," Frankie repeated.

"God-fucking-damn you, Seanie," she slipped into her pet name for her big brother as a preteen, before standing and going to the stage.

The microphone awaited Meghan on a stand. In front of her, a TV monitor waited on pause for her arrival. Frankie clicked his mouse, the video came to life, and music filled the rec room. The lyrics appeared on the screen and Meghan sang them.

Sean wasn't disappointed. His sister ripped into the lyrics, dumping whatever emotional baggage she may be carrying. Note for note, Meghan made the song her own, adding a keener's flair to extended and high notes. It was great, and Meghan stood poised to steal the show. A gracious round of applause from the audience made her blush a little, embarrassed by the attention. Meghan stepped away from the stage and returned to the table with Sean.

"Could I have Walt, Walt to the stage please?"

The old blind man, his cane outstretched before, waddled up to the mic stand. The timeless classic 'What A Wonderful World,' Louis Armstrong's version, came through the speakers.

Meghan sat and laughed.

Then Walt sang.

Sean put his finger over his lips to shush her.

He sounded like Armstrong reborn. A man, almost a century old, singing from his heart. Sean loved it. The melody enthralled not only him but all of the residents and family members in attendance. Everyone forgot about their troubles, as they experienced a spiritual cleansing.

"That's beautiful," Sean said during a vocal break. Meghan didn't answer, she waited, anticipating the remainder of the song. As it ended, Walt reminded each and every person there how wonderful the world truly was. After 99, or 96, years (*who's counting?*), he would know.

The karaoke faithful of SummerHome gave Walt a house-raising round of applause. RJ pulled his cheeks apart with his forefingers and wolf-whistled. Babs and Bill stopped making out long enough to participate. VIP Dave and Carry clapped with vigor along with the rest of the attendees. You could see the gratitude written in the wrinkles on his face.

Walt made his way back to his seat while the applause lingered. The DJ introduced another singer, calling up Island Tom, complete with a Hawaiian shirt, to sing some Jimmy Buffett.

"Oh, sure, make me follow up that," Tom joked when he took the microphone.

Sean recognized Tom from the Fenton Liquor store. The retiree still worked part-time there, selling spirits. The familiar chords of Margaritaville run through the speakers.

"He sings the same songs every week," RJ's companion said, irritated from hearing the song, "everyone does. Bobbie Be Good at least jazzed it up."

"Yes she did, Marion. Yes, she did," RJ's demeanor changed from one of excitement to remorse. Sean could see a tear roll down the custodian's cheek. "That's why I like this karaoke night, the DJ was working the night Bobbie disappeared. I miss her so much, still to this day."

"What happened to her?" Sean asked.

"She run off with some rock star," RJ said. Marion

cackled and shook her head.

"Ne-on-ah-yar-he took her. And him both," the old woman said.

"Ne-on-ah-yar-he?" Sean repeated the native word Marion spoke moments before, "What that?" The old woman had captured both Sean and Meghan's attention with this added flourish.

"A snow serpent that eats wayward men and loose women," RJ added, "Marion is an Onondaga Tribal Elder. She knows all the old myths."

"Yes, I do. Say? Have you ever heard of the flying head?"

"I can't say I have," Meghan responded. Sean shook his head and smiled.

"I have to know about this flying head," Sean said, "please, tell me about the flying head!" Meghan kicked Sean under the table.

"The *Ronearauyehne* came with the storms in spring and summer," Marion said, speaking with her hands as much as her mouth, "from the mountains to the east, terrorizing village after village throughout the Haudenosaunee. Some tribes called it the whirlwind, its wings creating the vortex upon which the thing flew. It would rend a person to pieces with its claws, then devour them, bones and all. Seeing this flying head was a bad omen, and usually foretold of death." Island Tom finished his song and Frankie called up Joey Soprano for some Sinatra. A portly older man with a ship's anchor tattoo on his forearm waddled up to the stage. His voice was a falsetto, higher than Sean ever heard a man sing. He wondered how he did it.

"There was a tribe in the mountains living on a remote lake," Marion continued, "no one remembers their name, but they were a prosperous people. After ages of living in harmony, a time of famine and drought came upon them and the lake water turned foul and undrinkable. This was followed by the harshest winter ever seen. When spring came, the young of the tribe decided it was time for the people to leave the mountains and live in the fertile hills. The tribe's elders refused to move, causing a rift between the young and the old." The old woman paused, sipped on her diet sprite, then continued with her tail after wetting her lips.

"The chief's son prayed to Tharonhiawakon, the god of creation and life, to save them, but the god's twin brother Tawiskaron, lord of snow and ice and creator of monsters, answered instead. He bade the Chief's son cut off the heads of the village elders and throw them in the lake and from this sacrifice he would save them from their plight."

"This is the scary part," RJ interjected. Marion wrinkled her brow and shook her head in disapproval of the interruption.

As if cutting off people's heads wasn't scary already? Sean thought.

"Yes, it's the scary part. Now, believing the demon, the Chief's son instructed his followers on what to do. They followed his direction, and beheaded their elders," Marion drew her wrinkly hand across her throat, "then the son placed all of the heads in a satchel, and threw it into the lake. The following night, as the tribe's survivors rested from preparing for their journey out of the mountains, something sinister rose from the depths, the flying head, a giant head with glowing red eyes and razor-sharp teeth. It flew on a pair of bat wings, and its short legs were crested with talons and claws." Marion hooked her bony fingers and clawed at the air with them.

"It attacked the murdering tribe folk, devouring them all in a single night. But it wasn't satisfied. It flew down from the mountains and attacked all of the villages in its path." In the limited lighting of the faux club, Marion's face seemed to transform into something otherworldly. Sean was surprised at how good of a storyteller the old woman turned out to be.

"When the Flying Head reached a Mohawk village, the villagers ran into hiding, all except for their Wise Woman, who refused to run. Instead, she sat at a campfire, roasting acorns. Ronearauyehne crept up on her, intending to devour the Wise Woman, but it stopped when it witnessed her eating the acorns. Believing she was eating the coals from the fire and in turn a god, the Flying Head flew away; back to the mountains in the east, not wanting to tangle with deities."

"That's it?" Sean said, underwhelmed with the climax.

"Yep," Marion said, and sucked on an ice cube from her drink. She had a tooth more than RJ. Franky announced last call for sign-ups, "myths are often anti-climactic. They're like shaggy dog stories, the best parts lead up to the end where nothing really happens."

"I guess so," Meghan said.

"Like many good myths," Marion continued, "it has a dual meaning. On one hand, it's a fable warning the elders to listen to their children," she paused again to suck up another ice cube, "and on the other, children shouldn't cut their parents' heads off for not listening to them." She cackled at her quip.

"I'm sorry folks," Frankie said, interrupting everyone, "the list is filled and I can't take any more requests tonight."

"Alrighty then!" Sean declared, taking advantage of the opportunity to leave. He worried he might hear another creepy myth if they stayed.

"Thank God. That was a sign from above to not sing,"

Meghan argued.

"Okay, then let's go," he said to her.

"What's wrong?"

"Nothing, it's been a long day with Mom and the outburst she had, I'd rather leave it at that. Good night Marion, goodnight RJ." Their neighbors nodded in response.

"Okay then, big brother. We shall be on our way," she said, and the siblings left SummerHome for the night.

CHAPTER 6: Dreams Come True

After karaoke, slinking unnoticed, the gray tabby cat wandered SummerHome and the stench of death followed. Throughout the halls and apartments, within the wake of the cat's path, nightmares blossomed. It weaved in and out of the shadows, awakening the fears within the subconscious of the sleeping residents.

The ghostly feline fed off the entropy of the dream world, the *other side* of the world we all know. The white diamond on its chest glowed in the darkness, pulsing as it manipulated the veil between these universes.

Take the Brooks in apartment twenty, for example. Carry, who now spelled her name Caryn, and whose real name was Karen, slept sound alongside her husband, David, affectionately dubbed the VIP by their neighbors.

Dave was called the VIP for a reason. The giant rocks on Caryn's fingers, as well as her Botox injections, were evidence of his deep pockets. In his younger days, this financial clout would give him advanced knowledge of fixed sporting events and the like, allowing him to amass a private fortune. He lived off this to this day. Being privy to advance knowledge of their imminent demise would have done anything to change the outcome.

As Carry got what Carry wanted, part of their deal with SummerHome was her pack of ankle-biting pug mixes. A soundproof front door later, so their neighbors couldn't hear their dogs, and they were residents. Their apartment sat at the back end of the facility, the furthest away from the other residents, which also helped with the barking.

All of this, because one night, Caryn's purse dog, her prize Pug bitch Miss Sassy, got out and whored around the streets of Fenton. A basset hound, a poodle, a pit bull, and a black lab suitor later; Miss Sassy came home bowl legged and knocked up. Two months later, a motley crew of puppies popped out of the little pug. Five ugly as sin, 'puppies,' with semi-anthropomorphic faces, snaggletooth underbites, and snot-filled noses. Caryn kept them all and named them after her grandkids.

There was no rhyme reason in their growth or coloring. One of them, Sammy, was yellow, like a traditional pug, but with a brindle pattern on his back end. He was already three times as big as the others.

This wouldn't be an issue, normally, except Sammy sat on his stool as he defecated. A forty-pound dog shits larger piles than a twelve or thirteen-pounder. Without fail, he'd end up with dog dirt sticking to his ass every time he'd squat.

The other dogs were better off. Two, Matty and Becky, had the curly locks of a poodle, with darker coats. The remaining pair, Timmy and Maxie, were spotted, with floppy ears. Add to this team their mother, Ms. Sassy, and you have a messed-up collection of dogs.

Dave couldn't stand them in the bedroom, so at night he gated them off in the apartment's kitchen. This prevented them from soiling the carpets. Dog beds and water bowls filled the kitchen area. A pair of baby gates bolted to the wall, held back Miss Sassy's brood.

They were a jumpy lot, always launching into the air, and Sammy was just plain big. As a result of this, Dave needed to use two gates, stacked one over the other, to contain them within the kitchen area. He covered the floor with piss pads, and let Carry deal with it when she would get up to make coffee in the morning.

Sometimes, the pissing dogs invaded Dave and Carry's dreams, barking away at the spectral cat they could sense outside their door.

Ignoring them, the cat continued on its rounds. It passed by apartment number eighteen, the door of Cindy

White. She went to karaoke at the rec center but didn't sing. Cindy participated in most activities at SummerHome to give her something to do.

She was a lonely woman. Cindy outlived her husband Paul by twenty years and never re-partnered. Most recently her only daughter, Katie, passed a few years ago. A successful nurse, Katie became the victim of a horrible murder in nearby Fulton.

A mother should never outlive her children, Cindy would say after news of her daughter's death reached her.

Two decades before, Cindy lost her teeth to gum disease brought on by smoking. Depressed over the loss of her husband, at first she refused dental treatment and dealt with the problems on her own. Cindy would find herself in the bathroom, pulling her loose teeth out of her mouth. She never forgot the pain, and neither did her nightmares, drawn out by the ghostly cat's presence.

Cindy stood in front of the mirror in the dreamscape bathroom. She didn't have to see it; her dreams knew she heard the pain. She's not implying the screams, as if she's been tortured in some manner or the audible snapping of a bone. No. Cindy's dreams remember the pain becomes audible when you rip your teeth out. She laughs when she sees people afraid of dentists, or the old movie with the Nazis in Brazil. Until you yank out a tooth-your own tooth-

with your fingers, you can't fathom the experience.

Cindy's nightmares know most people don't realize a tooth is still alive when you remove it. There are raw nerves attached to the roots, connecting them to your nervous system. When you pull on a loosey, every nerve ending cries out in agony, and you hear the fucking pain as you pull, yank, and twist to get it out of your mouth.

A person will do anything at this point to stop the agony lighting up the side of your face. The sleeping woman sees her dream-self reach into her mouth with two fingers. Her jaw screams with brilliant, tearing jolts, as the din of crashing metal in the outside world blends with her dream.

•

The cat passed by Babs and Bill's in apartment seventeen. The Drakes, fresh home from singing too many Cher songs, with and without Sonny, at the community center, were not immune to the nightmares within SummerHome on this night. They looked to be the doting couple in public, but decades of marriage can hide dark secrets. Babs could sleep like the dead, but Bill was a notorious sleepwalker, and one of the reasons they resided in SummerHome.

Typically, his sleepwalking was benign. On this

night, it took a dangerous turn. He rose from sleep, gently stirring Babs, who assumed he was going to the bathroom. She fell back to sleep.

Instead, he went to their kitchen and chain-smoked while he played with a butcher knife, stabbing their wooden carving board over, and over again.

Drawn out by the cat's presence, the hellish dreams flourished in the subconscious minds of each of SummerHome's sleeping residents, transforming as they progressed. They changed to nightmares, and then grew into night-terrors, dredging up the worst, most horrific memories the residents hid within, as the gray tabby cat passed by their doors. The nightmares, much like a thunderstorm, ended in a shower. Only these storms were anointed in blood and stained the ground crimson.

In apartment sixteen, Muriel Brownell's nightmares brought her back to the sexual abuse her now deceased ex-husband wrought on their family. Seeped in the regret of her inability to stop it, she still sees her daughter hanging from the rafter of their attic, the letter in her hands.

Muriel keeps this letter in her dresser.

Down the hall in apartment seven, Cheryl Huther's dementia-ridden dreams take her back to when she was a child. Her mother made her throw the robin eggs she found into the wooded lot behind their house. The first egg she threw cracked open in her hand, and the memory of the half-formed chick in the yolk imprinted on her.

A flock of adult robins attacked the young Cheryl in her dream. The songbirds' tiny talons and beaks, dripping in the girl's blood, rain on the lawn around her.

It's worth noting Cheryl never ate eggs again.

The robins attacking her didn't care. They pecked away at her, unrelenting in their determination to make her pay for her sin. Rivulets of blood sprayed out the wounds until there was none left in the host...

•

Joe Ryan, aka Joey Soprano, lived in number nine, the smallest apartment in the SummerHome facility, a studio near the boiler room. He lived there because the retired steelworker could handle the ambient heat. His memories of the forty years he worked at Crucible Steel popped back as he slept, and his body cinched into a fetal position on reflex.

Joe retired from the steel mill when they still gave pensions and, well, still operated out of Solvay. He worked there for forty years and only took a month off to recover from his surgery.

Like the summer of 1979. It's the only nightmare he

ever lived, the only memory to give him pause. And the cat drew it out of him like sweat.

It was a hot one, and it was hotter in the mill. Joe was a crane operator and had been running the bucket all day, pouring liquid steel from cauldrons into molds for reinforcement poles. The night before they ate at the Polish Home, and the cabbage wasn't settling well. He'd been a farting fool all day, stinking up his cab which was still 90 degrees with the air conditioning. Joe worried each time it struck him, he'd shit his pants at the mill before. The guys still hazed him about it, calling him Shitter Joe.

His break time came and Joe ran to the lavatory. A big man, weighing in at three hundred pounds, this was no easy feat for Joe to achieve, and he worked up more of a sweat. The heat covered his body in a sheen of perspiration. He hit the commode and liquid shit power washed the inside of the bowl, splashing his ass with cold toilet water. After a minute, when he was sure it was all out, he sat up to wipe his ass.

The toilet seat stuck to his thighs and rose with him. Annoyed, he sat back down. This was the day 'Shitter' Joe became 'Joey Soprano.'

Joe's testicles hung down under the seat, and when he sat back down, well, he more than pinched them. His sack got stuck to the bowl and stayed there. When he sat back down, almost his full body weight was focused on the front edge of the toilet seat, underneath which his balls rested.

His nuts popped and burst simultaneously with a splash of blood across his calves and ass cheeks.

Joe Ryan screamed so loud and shrill he lost his voice. When it came back, he could sing like a choirboy.

In the real world, Joe Ryan trembled, covered in sweat, as the memory haunted him. And it was the same for every door the cat passed. Through each occupied apartment in SummerHome, the dreams continued until the residents were startled awake by a disturbance.

While walking toward Walter Maddox's room, the cat stopped. Standing guard in front of the door stood an ethereal man in a German soldier's uniform from World War 2. The lightning bolts of the Wafen-SS stood out on his lapels. The spirit shook his head, a warning to the cat to stay clear of the room. The cat raised its haunches and hissed in defiance, the white diamond on its chest glowing fiercely. The musky stench of death filled the hallway, emanating from the spectral cat. Still, the spirit stood his ground, protecting old Walt from the influence of the cat.

Scheu kätzchen! The spirit's mouth says, with no words to follow. The spirit opens its maw wide, unhinging his jaw and revealing rows of coved fangs. The cat understands and warily obliges, stepping around the doorway, giving its guardian, the demonic ghost of SS-Hauptsturmführer Klaus Wagner, as wide a berth as possible.

•

A burning cigarette hung on Bill Drake's bottom lip. He hadn't smoked in decades, and it felt good going down, calming his frayed nerves. Their apartment was marked as a no smoking room, but he didn't care, he stood by the door, leaning against the wall, waiting for the nurse to arrive.

A large billow of smoke exited his lungs. The size of the cloud enveloping him gave Bill a chill to his bones. It was almost unnatural the amount of smoke as if a fog had blown into their room. And then it was gone, dissipating as he took another drag.

The nurse arrived and knocked on the door as Bill finished the smoke. The knocking was calm and slow. He chuckled. Maybe they didn't take him seriously.

Oh, you'll take me seriously in T-minus three or four seconds, he thought. Bill looked at his hands, some of the blood was still crusted under his fingernails.

Her blood. Babs' blood.

It would stain his hands forever, he supposed.

It didn't have to be this way, Bill reminded himself.

Babs did this. He heard keys rattle and the door opened.

"Mr. and Mrs. Drake, it's Dawn, your aid, you rang your alarm. Is everything okay? I'm coming in," a young woman in a nursing assistant's smock, her long brown hair pulled up in a high ponytail, opened the door and stepped into the apartment.

"Hello, Dawn," Bill greeted the CNA and took another drag off his cigarette.

"Hello, Mr. Drake," she said, "you know there's no smoking in here, right? You should put that out. Where's Mrs. Drake? Is she okay?"

"Not really, Dawn. Babs is dead."

"On second thought, don't put that out. Where is she? The bedroom?" she asked and he nodded, "I'm so sorry, Mr. Drake," she marched over to their bedroom.

"Me, too. I stabbed her while she slept," Bill said, nonchalantly, "sorry about the mess."

"You what?" she stopped in place before opening the door.

"I killed my wife," he repeated himself. Dawn pushed the bedroom door open revealing nothing out of the ordinary.

There was no scene of carnage. No blood. No bits and pieces of flesh and bone. No splatter pattern on the walls, rug, or bed. Babs lay in the bed, snoring away.

Bill couldn't believe his eyes. He knew he killed her.

He held the knife in his hands and stabbed it in her head. It popped like a grape. He could still smell and taste her blood. This couldn't be.

"Are you having another sleepwalking incident, Mr. Drake?" Dawn asked. The CNA knew their story. Both of the Drakes were sleepwalkers, and Bill started exhibiting dementia symptoms a few years ago. For safety's sake, the Drakes lived at SummerHome.

"What's going on? Bill, why is Dawn here?" Babs said, waking up.

"I think Bill pushed the alarm sleepwalking, Mrs. Drake, isn't that right Mr. Drake?" Dawn gave Bill a stern stare.

Don't you dare tell her what you told me; the CNA's eyes seemed to say.

"Yeah, yeah, that's right," Bill chuckled, "silly old Bill, sleepwalking again. And man, did I have a doozy of a nightmare this time. Wow."

"What was it about?" His wife asked.

"I don't remember," he lied.

A loud crashing sound from somewhere near the facility resonated throughout SummerHome and the Drakes' apartment.

"Probably a car accident on the main road. Okay, you two," Dawn interjected, "go back to bed. It's the middle of the night and I've got to go check on VIP Dave now."

"Of course, you do, he's the VIP, we wouldn't want to keep him waiting, now would we?" Bill said, still bewildered.

"No, not at all," the CNA said, smiling, and left the Drakes to themselves.

CHAPTER 7: Fencing

As nightmares spread through SummerHome, a yawn broke the silence in Dr. Abrahim Al-Mahairi's office. Karaoke was over, the residents were safely locked away in their apartments, and he could finally go home. He disliked the activity, so he hid in his office during the show. The walls barely kept the noise out, and always ground on his last nerve.

Tonight, though, was extra annoying, in part to the day's events. His cheek stung, and he winced. Abe sat behind his desk, the soft glow of his desk lamp the only light. He shifted papers, loading them into a satchel. He took a deep breath, wrinkled his nose, and nausea rose in his belly.

Something reeked.

A wretched stench of decay now filled the office. The doctor gagged. Spittle and mucus covering his lips. The stink reminded him of the resident's room earlier in the day.

Who was it? Oh, yes, Mrs. Coleman, the old racist and her dysfunctional children, he reminded himself, or, better yet, *how did she know I'm gay?* Abe never spoke of his private life, or his sexual orientation, and never around the residents. He wished for her to have another outburst so he could throw her out.

The clock on the wall in the doctor's office read 11:40 p.m. The position of Head Physician at SummerHome led to long days, such as this. Today was the first day of his midweek weekend. After leaving tonight he wouldn't be back for two days. He packed his bag at his desk, trying to detach from the burdens of his job, to leave them behind and not bring them home.

Abe's cheek, however, still throbbed from being clawed by Maureen Coleman. A grim reminder of how things can turn sour, and how difficult it is to leave the problems behind. He opened a bottle of aspirin, and took two, washing them down with the remaining contents of a water bottle.

He switched off his desk lamp, the ambient light from out his office window was enough to guide him out. He grabbed his work bag and stopped in place.

Al-Mahairi made a mental note to have the odor looked into when he got back. It was likely a sewage issue, and not frequent, otherwise, he'd have smelled it before. No longer wishing to deal with it, and wanting to get his well-earned two days off started, he stormed from his office.

The stench lingered in the hallway of SummerHome. None of the staff was in sight. With it being so close to 11:00, they were doing bed checks and shift change.

Then he remembered he failed to take his turn in the chess game with Walt. He rushed down the hallway. The wretched malodor thickened as each moment passed by. The hall lights flickered, then dimmed and brightened, before going out.

"This is great," Abrahim said to himself.

The lights flashed back on. The doctor remained in place, waiting to see if they clicked back off. They didn't.

The chess board in front of Walt's apartment sat unmolested, as it did every night. RJ knew to leave it alone. Abe assessed the situation and game state for a few minutes. Walt certainly put him in a bad spot. Any move he made would cost him a piece.

He finally resolved to protect his King and Queen and set up a Bishop for a sacrifice. He noticed the smell evaporated and took a deep breath. Shrugging his shoulders, he shook his head before heading to the employee exit.

The well-manicured grounds of SummerHome

welcomed Dr. Al-Mahairi. Surrounded by decorative, wrought iron fencing, and a lawn filled with bushes, the exterior of the facility resembled a redbrick Victorian garden.

He approached the secured gate and swiped his badge on a card reader. The security turnstile activated, and the chain-link fence to the parking lot slid open. He stepped through, placing a hand on the iron bars of the property fence.

A crackle of electricity precipitated a jolt of pain shooting up Abrahim's arm.

The shock took him by surprise, and Abe jumped back from the fence.

"What the fuck?" He said, shaking his hand to try and dull the pain. *What a day,* he thought, *it starts getting TKO'd by Granny MAGA, getting owned by a 100-year-old blind man in chess, and ends up getting electrocuted by a wrought iron fence.* If Abrahim Al-Mahairi ever needed a weekend, this day solidified the notion. He continued, being careful not to touch the fence.

Then he smelled it. The odor from within the facility. It permeated the air outside. It made him gag.

Abe clicked a button on his key fob, and the lights of his BMW 3 Series flashed. He hurried to his car, opened the door, and threw his bags in as he threw himself into the driver's seat. He slammed the door and jammed the key into the ignition. The engine fired up, and Abe turned off the exterior vents and turned on the car's air conditioning. Cold air blasted out onto his face, taking the nausea away.

He didn't bother putting his seatbelt on, opting instead to jam the car into drive and flick the lights on. His foot pressed the accelerator, and the car sped off, squealing tires in the process.

It's not a good idea to drive past, say, ten or fifteen miles an hour in a parking lot. You could hit another car, for example. Or a person. A car going forty miles an hour in a parking lot is, at the least, careless of the driver.

Abrahim Al-Mahairi didn't give a fuck.

He pressed the pedal to the floor, and by the time his BMW reached the threshold of the property line, he was doing forty, easily. This happens with a car capable of going from a standstill to sixty miles an hour in about eight seconds.

The problem with reaching forty miles an hour in a sedan in a parking lot is when you hit an iron fence, bad things happen. You see, the fence will always win this battle. You're not going fast enough to knock the fence over. The wrought iron will stop the car dead in its tracks, and a BMW with a hundred and fifty-four horsepower engine is no different.

A forward collision with the fence will do a number on the car's front end. A trip to the body shop will be warranted. A new grill, new plastic, and fiberglass parts will be required.

The occupant of the vehicle, once hitting the fence, in theory, should end up okay. After all, they're restrained in their seat, with an airbag deployment to protect them, right? Everything is in place to survive the collision with little more than whiplash as a reminder.

Unless you gave fuck-all about putting your seatbelt on. In which case, all of the rest is moot and you become a meat projectile.

Time gave Dr. Abrahim Al-Mahairi about a third of a second to wonder where the fence came from before he launched through the windshield of his Beamer, face first. He failed to deduce the former, as he smashed into the fence's bars.

Stationed eight inches apart, the bars prevented potential wandering residents from leaving the property. Tonight, they provided the perfect device to smash through flesh and bone. When EMTs arrived fifteen minutes later, they discovered Dr. Abrahim Al-Mahairi stuck into the fence, up to his shoulders.

His head jutted out the other side of the barrier. The flesh on the sides of his face was peeled back by the impact of sliding through the fence. The bones within his skull shattered on impact, allowing his swelling brain to burst out of either side of his head, dripping with cranial fluid. Bits of skull, like a broken eggshell, still clung to the gray matter by the time the ambulance arrived.

If Dr. Al-Mahairi lived, he might have commented on the return of an all too familiar stench surrounding the accident scene; it followed him throughout the day. The paramedics smelled it through their facemasks. The odor was nothing new to them.

The smell of death.

•

Inside SummerHome, The residents, nurses, and aides heard about the accident. For the most part, none of the residents knew what happened. Those who knew amongst the night shift CNAs and nurses on duty wouldn't say anything until the next day. The cat may have heard the racket, but it didn't indicate it had. The ethereal feline ended its rounds and returned to its home, if ghostly cats would have such a place, in Maureen Coleman's bedroom.

Deep asleep within her apartment, the ruckus didn't wake Maureen from her slumber, but her subconscious heard the collision and found pleasure in the sound. Bundled into bed with the gray tabby cat now curled up next to her, and purred while Maureen subconsciously smiled.

She woke the next morning with a smile still on her face.

CHAPTER 8: Butterflies

The Coleman family home sat on the outskirts of Fenton, off Rt 104 near Lake Ontario. A two-story colonial with a half dozen bedrooms and four full baths, the property was well maintained, with a luscious butterfly flower garden. The Colemans, and the Spencers, and the Cunninghams before them, had lived here since anyone in Cayuga county could remember. Sean and Meghan knew it was considered a Historical Location, and they needed approval from the Historical committee to do any work on the property.

Once inside their house, brother and sister went straight to their bedrooms. Sean's head hit his pillow, thinking about the weird story old Marion told at karaoke. Within minutes, he fell into his typical dreamless slumber.

Meghan's room, on the other side of the house, overlooked the backyard of the property. On this night, she found her bed to be her most comfortable experience in recent memory. With all the stress of moving her mother, and now her health deteriorating at a higher rate of speed than anyone anticipated, she needed to unplug and recharge. Meg turned off her phone, took a shower, and crawled under the sheets. She fell asleep in moments.

•

A loud collective gasp, followed by the clanking of metal cutlery on ceramic plates, filled the hallway of her home. She scanned the area, looking for anything out of the ordinary and saw Rosella.

Meghan knew her name was Rosella, and she was the groundskeeper's wife. She ran straight down the hallway to the kitchen, huffing and panting away as she did.

"What happened? What's going on?" Meghan asked the woman. She bent over, catching her breath.

"Come to the garden and see it for yourself. God," the woman grasped the crucifix hanging around her neck, "Papiyon! Papiyon!" Rosella said, before she fell to her knees, shaking, and made the sign of the cross.

What did she say? Meghan didn't understand the language. Was it Spanish? No, it wasn't. Then what was it?

"*Vini avèk mwen koulye a!*" Rosella shouted, "No pawol Kreyol? Come with me, now! It's *mirak*! A miracle!"

Instead, she follows the woman out the pantry door in the back of the house. A strong, pungent flowery aroma filled the air. When they arrived, Meghan couldn't believe her eyes.

Thousands of winged insects, moths, and butterflies fluttered throughout the daisy garden and Mountain Ash bushes, their yellow flowers blooming bright.

"Do you smell that? It smells like-" Rosella said before Meghan interrupted.

"Roses, Rosella. It smells like a big bouquet of roses."

A cloud, painted with the wings of the butterflies engulfed Meghan. The flying insects encircled her, moving faster until they created an isolated tunnel in the garden, with a sole occupant.

Meghan.

A giant, black and gold Monarch butterfly hovered in the air in front of her face, and she saw the image from the photograph unfold before her. The flash of a camera, an old Polaroid, in Rosella's hands and a photographic image growing on the film.

Then the insects were gone. Meghan and Rosella still stood in the garden, but the butterflies were gone. The sky grew dark, and Rosella's features warped.

"The fondest memories are saved first," Rosella said,

her accent shifting with her appearance. Darkness and shadows fell across the garden and Rosella's form faded away.

In her place stood a red-haired lass in an 118th-centurydress and bonnet. Rain fell from the sky. Young Meghan looked at it covering her. It touched her lips and tasted different. Rain was salty, this had a tinge of copper to it. She opened her eyes. The rain was crimson. Red and pink dots covered her white dress. The girl screamed for her mother.

No one came.

·

Meghan thrashed on the bed in her sleep, sweat beading on her forehead and matting the hair to her face. She finally woke from the dream, gasping for her breath. How could she know she witnessed someone else's nightmare? Or it would soon be her own?

"The fondest memories are saved first," a chorus of voices repeated, thick with rolling Irish accents.

These nightmares, new to her psyche, were fair on this, their opening night. They let her get some rest, hidden behind the echoes of falling rain.

Crimson rain...

CHAPTER 9: Shit Ball

A cloud of gray smoke filled the facade on top of Donahue's Furniture warehouse. The Haunted Mansion smelled of tobacco and skunks. Obscured within its confines, a trio of men stood in a semi-circle, smoking a fat blunt stuffed with marijuana. The morning wake and bake, the crew called it. They all arrived at work early to practice this daily ritual.

Sean took the wrap from Miz and sucked in a giant hit. Frank, aka Ron Franklin, another of the furniture handlers, waited patiently for his turn. Sean was lost in thought, thinking about his mother and the outburst she had the other day. Seeing her in this condition broke his heart.

"Hey Spence, where's Timmy and Willy?" Frank asked, referring to the other handlers on shift, Gene

Timmons and Norm Wilson.

"The carpet truck came early, so they're down in the bay with Gorman. We'll leave the clip up here for them. Don't worry," Sean said.

"I heard the ghost of Jim Donahue saved your life the other day," Miz said.

"Yeah, I had to pick that mess up. You're lucky none of the chairs got busted," Frank faked anger.

"But none did. Thanks for the assist."

"Anytime, bitch," Frank took the blunt from Sean. He took a deep drag on it and started coughing.

"So did you guys hear what happened to Ron?" Miz changed the subject, "He took that chair out on a solo delivery in Fair Haven yesterday. Homeowner dude answers the door wearing nothing but a jockstrap."

"That's fucking hilarious," Sean laughed out. Frank tried to laugh, but he only coughed more.

"Ron didn't think so. He asked the guy to put on some pants." Miz continued.

"I'm sure he did," Sean winked, "He'll tell the priest the truth at confession this Sunday."

"Well, I walked in on Gollum and Elvis," this revelation caused eyebrows to raise, "I'd almost rather trade places with Ron. I'm still having nightmares from it," the other guys chuckled at the factoid, but it was only partially true.

Sean couldn't recall ever having a dream, at least any he remembered. He knew he did dream, everyone dreamed-it was a scientific fact, but Sean never recalled any, ever. Since seeing her naked, visions of Gladys O'Connor as Gollum ran rampant through his waking thoughts, making them walking nightmares. Recalling the visual made him nauseous.

It fucks us good, me precious!

"Yeah, I met my mother's neighbors, the O'Connors," Sean added.

"They were role-playing?" Miz stifled a snicker as he spoke.

"You could say that," Sean covered his eyes with his hands, "It was rather, um, revealing?"

"I wonder who he'll dress up as next time?" Frank asked.

"At least I think he was supposed to be Elvis," Sean answered in his best Elvis voice. The group laughed.

"You better be careful, the old lady might want her old man to be the furniture delivery man next," Miz ribbed. Sean turned pallid. Mention of the old lady in any manner of nudity brought back visions of Gollum in a hardcore porno.

Fuck me, my precious! Fuck me harder! HARDER! Spence heard her creepy fucking voice invade his head, again. It gave life to a full-on hallucination of the old hag bent over, her flaccid tits swaying back and forth.

For him, this visual was fast becoming the Gilligan's Island theme of mind fucks, the ultimate mental earworm. He half expected Gladys Gollum to pop out from behind Frank and Miz, her mouth open and drool seeping out of her lips and toothless gums. But instead, something else caught everyone's attention.

"Isn't this at that SummerPlace or whatever it's called?" Frank asked.

"SummerHome," Sean corrected him.

"Yeah, yeah, SummerHome. I saw on the news before I came in this morning, some doctor there had a car accident last night."

"What?" Sean pulled out his cell phone to check the news. There it was, a headline giving all the details he needed.

SUMMERHOME DOCTOR, DEAD AFTER FREAK ACCIDENT

"Yeah, it's weird," Frank said, "the video footage on the news was pretty rough. Front end of the car was smashed in and it looked like he went through the windshield and hit the fence, too."

Sean saw the pictures and grimaced. Then he noted the name.

Abrahim Al-Mahairi.

His mother's doctor.

"What the fuck!" Sean yelled as the flooring of the facade shook. His bones could *feel* a muffled sound, rattling up through the building's frame. Frank continued to cough and gag.

"Jesus, Frank, take a drink, or something," Sean yelled at him, trying to figure out the source of the shaking.

"The more you cough, the more you get off, Spence." His coughing trailed off.

"Yeah, yeah, whatever. You guys feel that?"

"Feel what?" Miz asked as he stubbed out the cherry on the blunt.

The building groaned, a deep wailing reverberating through the bricks, mortar, and steel. It resembled the roar of a Toho movie monster. And sent a shiver up the spine of all three men.

"What the fuck. Is that the ghost of Mr. Donahue?" Miz asked. Sean could see the goosebumps rising on Miz's arms.

"You mean the ghost of Mr. Fitzgerald," Frank corrected him.

"This was Donahue's walking stick, not Fitzgerald's," Miz rolled his eyes.

"That, however, wasn't a ghost," Sean added, "the last time I heard a sound like that was at my family camp up in Clayton. It came from the septic system. Um, we better go downstairs." Sean didn't have to tell Miz and Frank to move, they already spooked themselves to the elevator with the ghost talk and the fallen walking stick.

•

Meghan Coleman sorted through the clutter stored in the attic. Between daily visits with Mom, cleaning the house, and working, Meghan had absolutely no time for herself, except sleep. The latter wasn't always easy to accomplish, and when she did, it was riddled with random blurs of dreams, curtained by a shower of crimson rain.

She found a dusty hat box and opened it, revealing hundreds of old color photographs scattered within. Meghan wondered why they never made it into one of Mom's many photo albums. A picture on the top of the stack caught her eye. It featured a young, pre-teen girl standing in the arched flower garden in their backyard.

The picture from her dream. A young woman with a gold and black butterfly on her nose.

Set in the center of a grove of trees in the backyard of their house, the garden held a trove of pleasant memories of her childhood.

She and Mom took walks there often and found

themselves in the garden often. A myriad of aerial insects buzzed about and flew around them, Meghan remembered chasing the butterflies and running from the bees. A memory now fresh as if it happened the day before.

Because it did.

A big black and gold Monarch hovering in the air next to her, captured in time by the magic of still photography. But outside of the dream, her mind played out the night before, Meghan possessed no recollections of this day. The memory lapse caused her to panic. She feared she too would fall into Alzheimer's at an early age. It's obvious it happened. She dreamed about the memory, then she saw the picture. It must have happened.

"This isn't fair!" Meghan screamed out, keeping the rest of her thoughts inside. She wept. Her tears fell from her face and created miniature mud balls on the dusty wooden planks of the attic floor. She stared at the pictures in the box. All of these pictures were memories captured in time. Each one a memory the living Maureen Coleman lost daily as her brain shrunk and shriveled and died in her skull.

Why my mother? Why Maureen Coleman? Why take her mind before taking her body? Why not take her all at once? She didn't do anything to deserve this hell she's living in now!

Why me?

"Fuck you, God!" She cursed aloud. Meghan put the picture down, closed the box, and pushed it to the side with others she planned to keep. Her red hair stuck to her wet face and lips, getting into her mouth. She brushed it aside and moved on to the next box.

This box contained a menagerie of papers, everything from greeting cards to newspaper clippings and legal papers. Why some of these papers weren't in a lockbox somewhere baffled Meghan. The topmost papers, the vet bill for her cat's euthanasia, brought a tear to her eye, souring the moment.

What were you thinking, Mom? She thought and shook her head. Her mother saved every birthday card, anniversary card, and holiday card she ever received from anyone. This would be another box to sort through later, like the photographs. Meghan's sense of nostalgia and curiosity demanded items of this nature be preserved, not discarded in boxes in an attic.

•

Sean stopped the elevator car on the second floor at the loading docks. A foul stench greeted them, beating away the typical *od du elevator.* It smelled like someone burned diarrhea batter cupcakes with shit frosting. His eyes watered and his stomach lurched in revulsion.

"What a way to start a day, for fuck's sake," Sean remarked.

"For fucking real," Frank said.

When the door opened, the malodor hit them full-on. Frank pulled his shirt over his face. Miz stopped at the threshold, hacked, and spit up a mouthful of bile down into the elevator trap, adding to its vile mixture. Sean wondered if the stink and noise might be related. If anyone knew the answer, it would be Gorman, and the last they knew, the man was on two, around the corner, unloading the carpet truck.

Miz ran off to the shop, in the other direction, drool hanging from his lips. Sean and Frank didn't expect to see Gorman behind the wheel of the crashed tow motor, its fork track wedged into a giant, two-inch-thick steel pipe in the ceiling. A large puddle of a foul-smelling, black ichor surrounded the crash site. It resembled greasy dark chocolate pudding. Sean wished he had his phone to take a picture of this.

"Now push when I say," Gorman commanded, "and...

now! Push!"

Timmons and Wilson stood in the puddle of whatever-it-was. Their feet slipped and slid in the goo as they attempted to push the tow motor. Gorman floored the forklift in reverse, its wheels burning rubber on the concrete floor.

It didn't budge.

Another groaning sound emanated from the pipe. It seemed to come from the very bowels of the structure. The pipe vibrated.

"This can't be good. You two, move, now!" Gorman ordered his subordinates. Timmy and Willy didn't waste a second running away. Gorman fought with his safety belt on the tow motor. The accident jammed the mechanism, and the metal wouldn't give.

"Gorman, come on!" Sean shouted to the foreman.

"Sweet fucking Jesus," Gorman said. Unable to leave the driver's seat, he dropped his sunglasses over his eyes and held onto the bars of the tow motor's roll cage.

Sean and the other warehouse employees watched as the pipe jiggled, rattled, and vomited a basketball-sized lump of shit out of its jagged opening. Accumulating for years in the pipes of the building, the blow to the main pipe shook it loose from where it nested. The massive, gelatinous glob of crap hit Chris Gorman square in the face, exploding on contact.

A splatter of tenderized, fermented human waste formed a ten-foot circle of feces around the forklift. It filled the docking bay with a noxious odor. The impact knocked Gorman out cold.

A mental image entered Sean's head, of how he could replicate the sight before him. The process required a few boxes of lumpy brownie mix, some German Chocolate cake batter, a few gallons of Chocolate sauce, and the air surrounding a dairy farm. But this isn't what he saw when his eyes returned to the scene.

Sean couldn't focus his eyes. They stopped working together. One didn't move, the other quivered before it turned to stare at the haze hanging over the tow motor. He closed them, but when he opened his eyes back up, they remained out of sync.

What's going on, what the fuck am I witnessing? Sean thought. His one eye saw more than shit dripping from the broken pipe. *An essence flowed out.* It surrounded Gorman's body, engulfing him, entering through his nose and mouth.

Sean closed his eyes one more time and shook his head vigorously. He opened them to find them working as a tandem pair, again. The ether cloud, too, disappeared. Gorman's body convulsed as his diaphragm came to life.

The warehouse foreman woke up, and responded by

vomiting, adding his lunch to the rest of the shit. The other handlers stood in awe, not knowing what they should do. In lieu of doing nothing, they broke out in ill-advised nervous laughter. Gorman stopped gagging long enough to take his sunglasses off and respond to the heckling. A white ring of flesh surrounded his eyes, turning him into a scatological raccoon, which made the secession of said laughter a little more difficult for the parties involved.

"Would somebody call 911 and get me an ambulance, please! And the rest of you bozos? You can clean this-" he stopped, looking for the right words, "this, this shit up! Literally!"

"I'll call the ambulance. Do they need the jaws of life?"

"Fuck you, Spence, just make the fucking call!" Gorman screamed, globs of runny shit streaming down his face, dripping into his mouth. He gagged spit-up, and flipped Sean the bird. Gorman flicked a wad of poop off his finger in the process. It smacked Timmons between the eyes. He dry heaved on impact.

"What the fuck, Gorman!" He managed to retort between spasms.

Sean hopped on the elevator before any crap found its way to him. He looked at his watch. In an hour he was clocking out and going to visit Mom and deal with

Lord knows what from his sister.

CHAPTER 10: Just Another Day

A pot of boiling pasta rolled on the stove in Maureen Coleman's apartment at SummerHome. Meghan Coleman stirred the spaghetti. Next to it, a saucepan simmered with a meaty red sauce gravy. The delicious aroma of garlic and oregano filled the rooms and leaked into the hallway.

Standing next to the stove at the kitchen counter, Meghan and Maureen worked in tandem, slicing up squid and breading it for a calamari side dish with dinner.

"I'll fry the calamari when Sean gets here," Meghan said.

"That will be nice," Maureen replied, "did you get it in town?"

"Yes, actually. At Price Chopper."

"Oh, you could have gotten it fresher from Bella."

"Bella's? Is that a seafood place? Or a new Italian

restaurant?" Meghan asked her mother.

"New Italian restaurant where?" Maureen replied.

"Bella's?" Meghan said. She saw her mother's eyes stare off and Meghan understood what happened.

"Who? What?" Maureen asked in return, her eyes staring blankly past Meghan at something behind her. She turned around, and nothing was there, aside from her bedroom.

She couldn't see the gray tabby cat watching and listening from the recesses of Maureen's bedroom, hidden in the shadows.

It became obvious to Meghan the Alzheimer's might be the problem. She changed the subject.

"It's horrible about the doctor, mom," Meghan said. The news of the accident spread quickly through the media. Meghan learned of the tragedy through the drive home radio news on her way to SummerHome.

"Brownies," she shook her head, "they ain't too bright, you, know, the dumbest of the lot. They're all pretty easy to trick, though. I should know. Do you know something else? They're really only good at cleaning houses. You saw how bent they get when you insult them."

"Mom, please, stop with the racist talk."

"Okay then, the fair-"

"Mom," Meghan interrupted her mother, "Please!

Maybe we shouldn't talk about the doctor. I might find a nice Italian man if I keep cooking like this," Meghan changed the subject.

"No half-breeds in our family," Maureen replied. She sat next to the kitchen in her reclining chair, watching her daughter cook them dinner.

"Mom, that's not nice. What's gotten into you?"

"Neither are the Guineas. Greasy little bastards. You can't trust them one bit. But they do make good food."

"What did I just say about being racist? Good Lord!"

"I wasn't being racist before. But I guess I am now," Maureen's casual manner about it came out deadpan. Meghan shook her head and ignored her mother's xenophobic comments.

Instead, she went about setting the table for plates and silverware for three people. She looked at the clock, it said four-thirty, Sean should be here any moment now. He knew Mom insisted on eating dinner with them. They made it part of the deal when they brought Mom to SummerHome. His being this late couldn't be called typical by any means, but since moving the family dinners here from home, it looked to become the norm.

Meghan tested a strand of spaghetti. It resisted her bite ever so slightly, a perfect al dente. She turned off the burner, strained the spaghetti, and ran cold water over it. She'd give the sauce a few more minutes. She helped her mother over to the dinner table.

"Mom, I wanted to ask you about something I found at the house today," Meghan said as she guided her mother from the reclining chair to the table chair.

"What is it?" Maureen sat down at her plate.

"I found a box of pictures in the attic today. And old papers."

"Is that so?"

"Yes, anyways, I found this old picture of the flower garden and trestles." Meghan's quilted purse sat on the table next to her plate. She retrieved the photograph she found and put it on the table in front of her mother.

"That's pretty. I think I remember that day. Gosh, it was so long ago."

"Why were these in the attic?"

"Why not? I put a lot of things in the attic for storage over the years. Can I keep this picture? Could you put it on the refrigerator door?"

"I sure can, Mom," moments like this, when Meghan could see her mother's spark, were becoming fewer. A tear grew in the girl's eye as she placed a magnet over a corner of the old photo and attached it to the fridge's white surface.

"I'm going to the bathroom."

"Right now?" Meghan opened her eyes wide in shock.

"Well, yes," Maureen replied, "I'm not going, *going*

right now. I'm losing my marbles, not my bladder control. I'm going to the commode and then I'll go, *go*."

"Okay, I get it," Meg couldn't help but laugh as Maureen walked to the bathroom, and closed the door behind her.

•

A summer rain storm, complete with hail, thunder, and lightning, caused traffic problems in Fenton. Visibility in the downpour was at a bare minimum, making the streets a sea of red brake lights. As a result, Sean arrived at SummerHome later than he anticipated. His stress level was through the roof and he shook with a nervous twitch. He parked, and ran inside the facility, getting soaked in the process and irritating him more. Water dripped off him as he walked down the hallway, leaving behind a trail of water. He noted old man Walt sitting in front of his apartment, once again staring off blankly in front of a chess game.

One that would never be finished, Sean noted to himself, still shocked about Dr. Al-Mahairi's untimely passing.

"Good evening Walt," Sean said, greeting the old man.

"Good evening, John."

"Sean, I'm Sean."

"I know you; I know you think your name is Sean. Sean is Irish for John; did you know that?"

"Yes, I did, as a matter of fact."

"That makes you a John in my book."

"I guess it does, sir," the men chuckled together, "it's a shame about the Doctor."

"Yes, yes it is," Walt concurred.

"Your game, too, I guess is over."

"I wouldn't say that. The most important piece on the chess board is the General, it's not a real piece, it's the guy moving the pieces. The General tells everyone, from the pawns right up to the King and Queen, what to do on the battlefield. So, is this battle over? No. Are we in need of a general? I'd say we are."

"That's a good point, Walt. I guess we'll have to see who takes up the mantle for the Black King and Queen."

"I guess we will. It's Black's turn now. The Doctor, he baited me with a sacrifice on his last turn. Seems kind of inappropriate and disrespectful for me to take it now. So, I just castled instead. This is a gentleman's game, after all. At least Klaus thinks so."

"Who's Klaus?"

"The Nazi I shot in the head back in 1944."

"That's right, I think I heard the story. You're pretty

legendary around here, hah?"

"If you say so, Klaus is the chess player, he's the general, not me. He guides my hand, has since I shot him. Says he's waiting for me to move on. He doesn't want to go to Hell for following orders, not yet."

"Is that so? That's pretty creepy if you ask me. Well, that, and that you've got your own personal ghost or something like that?" Sean played along with old Walt's delusion.

"I do," Walt said and nodded, "no different than your own mother, I've heard. News travels fast here at SummerHome."

"I guess so. Well, goodnight," Sean said, hoping the tone of his voice didn't betray his skeptical opinion of Walt's invisible Nazi companion, "I'm going to see my Mom and sister."

"Tell Maureen old Walt Maddox says hi."

"I will," Sean shook his head and smiled. He liked Walt, and talking with him calmed his nerves, if for but a moment. The old blind crooner held a century of wisdom in his head, and a ghost advisor if the stories were true.

•

ean burst into his mother's apartment without a word, his face now covered in a scowl as his shitty day came back to haunt him. Meg rushed to meet her brother.

"What is your problem?" She whispered to him.

"You have no idea what I've gone through today."

"Well, you're tweaking like a meth head. Stop it."

"I am not. But I am nervous and anxious as fuck, Megs."

"Get over it. Mom will see it."

"Are you my sister or my fucking wife? Note I am single and don't have a wife. Why? Because I don't like this bullshit. Jesus. Who cares if she sees me shaking?"

"Her doctor died last night; did you know? She's a little weird about it, too."

"Yeah, I heard. What the fuck happened to him?"

"I guess he ran his car into the fence and got ejected through the windshield. I heard it was pretty ugly. Now, look like you want to be here," Meghan poked her brother in the side.

"Alright, already." Sean complied and walked with at least some form of confidence, "Yeah, I'm glad to be here," Sean lied, "sucks about the doctor."

"Our mother has mixed-dementia symptoms from early-onset Alzheimer's, which led to us bringing her here for residency. This is never a tough decision. I've been fine with it. I don't feel the stress of tending to her for extended periods any longer. Now we can visit daily, and have quality time together," she waited for him to contribute to the conversation.

"I've had a shit day, Meg. This isn't the time."

"Try me."

"Do you really want to know how I feel?" He shook his head as he spoke.

"I don't know, do I? What is it, Sean?" Meghan asked her brother, an expression of concern growing on her face.

"Okay, I'll tell you. It's sucked. Okay? Like, really, really sucked. The other day, a tower of chairs almost crushed me. Then I learned our mother's mental state is worse than we first thought. I watch her scratch her doctor in the fuckin face. Today my boss ripped open a sewage pipe and spread shit all over the loading dock I work on. I swear I saw a fucking ghost come out of the pipe and perform the fucking Heimlich Maneuver on Gorman. And all of this is going on two weeks after you strong-arm me into putting our Mom in a home!"

"Is that how you feel? That I strong-armed you?" Meghan interrupted him.

"Didn't you? It was SummerHome or bust if I recall."

"Jesus, Seanie, It's not like this is a hospital room with nothing but a bed and a curtain. She's got her own apartment!"

"It doesn't matter. I'm actually over all that, now. If she's sick and getting worse, this is the best place for her, with doctors and nurses if she needs them. Plus, she has peers here."

They heard the toilet flush.

"Okay. Enough. You win, I'm not arguing with you here, today, in front of Mom. Let's sit down, please."

"I thought you learned your lesson about knocking," Meghan asked her brother.

"First you get in my face without a hello, and now you want to bring back memories of what can't be unseen."

"You did it, not me."

"Bullshit, you followed me in."

"And I followed you out, too."

"What are you two talking about," Maureen interjected as she left the bathroom.

"The other day we accidentally walked in on your neighbors," Sean revealed to his mother, making something up to change the subject. Meghan crossed her arms and stared her brother down.

"We?" she asked with a stern tone.

"Yes, we," he sat down at his spot at the table, "sorry I'm late, let's eat, I'm starving, and do I have a story to tell you two. Is that deep-fried calamari I smell?" Sean declared. Maureen sat, too, as Meghan served them dinner.

Sean told the story of Gorman eating a shit football, omitting the ghost part. It might not have been an entirely appropriate dinner conversation, but it was a family dinner. To Meghan and Sean, every remaining family dinner they shared with their mother was a cherished moment, regardless of the subject matter. Besides, a good shit joke is always good for a laugh or two, to make you forget how smeared in crap things are.

Sean and Meghan tucked their mother into bed, then left, walking together to their cars. Sean noticed Walt's chess board, sitting on the table in the hallway. The man had long since gone to bed. Sean walked over to it.

"What are you doing?" Meghan asked.

"Taking the dead Doctor's turn," Sean replied.

"Why?"

"Because it's the right thing to do," Sean examined the board and noted Walt was correct. A bishop was left in jeopardy on the board. But Walt's castling gave Sean the chance to move the Bishop out of harm's way, and he did so.

"Take that, Klaus!" Sean said.

"Is that it?" Meghan asked. He nodded, and sat up from the chair, then escorted his sister to her car before following her home, as he always did.

After her kids left, Maureen Coleman stared at the wall, watching the shadows cast by her bedroom window. She relished the bliss of her children coming over, and for the first time since she moved here, Maureen felt at home.

When John Magee's spirit reappeared, it stole her happiness and filled the void with doom.

The time is nigh for ye to join the others, his ghastly lips mouthed the words none could hear.

"No. We- I'm- not ready," Maureen protested, "I'm not ready to move on, don't you see?"

'Tisn't for ye to make this decision. The process has begun. The ghost of John Magee disappeared in the same manner as it arrived, evaporating without any fanfare.

The spirit told the truth. Since before she came here, Maureen's memories were fading. Of them, those Maureen never experienced firsthand, because they were not her own, went first. What others saw as dementia, Maureen saw as taking back her mind and body after over forty years of sharing it with a host of ancestral matriarchs.

It's like a hive of hornets in my head, Moira told her, referring to the half-dozen personalities sharing her brain.

Unlike Maureen and Meghan, Moira Cunningham prepared her daughter for the event. Young girls typically have a trio of 'talks' with their mother. Puberty is a catalyst for them, starting with their first monthly, then the typical birds & the bees discussion, culminating with the teenage pre-marital sex warning. The girls in Moira's family tree trunk added one more, a subject breached when she reached maturity: *The Transference.*

The tradition of doing this went back seven generations until Maureen broke it with no intent of her own. The time for her Transference came early and unannounced. One day, Maureen went to bed, and she woke up wandering in the field next to their home.

Seven generations, using the isolated gene pool required for the Fae magic, led to genetic defects and early onset Alzheimer's. First her stroke, then the disease. The tandem caused Biddy and the others living in Maureen's head to hide in the depths of her mind, away from its poison. This left Maureen in charge of her faculties, which led to perceived personality changes in her demeanor.

Her family was right when they attributed this to the disease. It brought out Maureen's old personality,

complete with that person's memories. But now it didn't
matter. Hell, Maureen knew nothing ever mattered, to
begin with.

CHAPTER 11: Dark Memories

The war hero and karaoke crooner Walter Maddox, 97 years young, blind as a bat with hearing just as good, went to bed soon after chatting with Maureen Coleman's son.

John. Sean. Jean. Jack. Giovanni. It's all the same name. They're all the same. And Walt knew, or knew of, them all in the century he'd spent on this planet. Walt had a good ear; it came with being blind. He heard things most people didn't catch on to. For example, he never saw a ghost, but he sure could sense them.

The air shimmered and vibrated whenever Klaus came around. Walt couldn't see it, but he could feel it, hear it. Walt guessed the old Nazi's spirit was tied to the jacket and scarf. He couldn't see him now, he never did, and this included the days when Walt could still see, but he could always tell when the old German ghost was there. It was Klaus who guided his hand when they played chess.

Hell, it was Klaus who woke him up on the morgue ship. The memory haunted Walt for decades. They called it PTSD today, but back in Walt's day, you called it anything but what it was. Vodka. Heroin. The names changed but the damage remained.

"If only he knew what I know now, poor kid," Walt said. He prided himself in never forgetting a person he met. After losing his eyesight to the sugar, with Klaus there to help point out the nuances, he learned to identify them by their voices. And Maureen Coleman wasn't who she claimed to be. Walt heard something different in her voice.

No.

He heard someone *else* in her voice. He knew the voice, and it belonged to someone he heard long ago before he went to the war.

Walt fancied himself a ladies' man back in his youth, a war hero fresh home from the war. He made it with quite a few women in Fenton. He was light-skinned and straightened his hair best as he could so he could pass for a white man if not under scrutiny. He had to fess up when he went into the Army, but by the time Walt was drafted, the Army had integrated. Oh, and his pecker hung down to his knee.

Oh yes, young, virile, and attractive, Walt Maddox got all the pussy.

The mother of the Cunningham girl, Moira was her name, she was a horny old cougar and Walt remembered when she sucked him off in the back of the old movie theater before her last name was Cunningham.

Moira spoke with a particular cadence to her voice, and Walt heard it in her, and he heard it in her daughter Molly. He fucked her after the war and a night drinking at the Harbor Festival. And he heard it from Molly's daughter.

Maureen Coleman.

His current neighbor at SummerHome.

Walt never fucked Maureen Coleman, or Spencer as she was before Jack Spencer died. No, he didn't want anything more to do with their crazy family, and besides, he was too old for her by then.

What didn't settle as well with Walt was hearing the other voice come out of Maureen's daughter when she spoke. It gave him the creeps and bugged him more than his experiences in World War II. Bugged him more than Klaus's near-constant presence.

He turned over in bed, and his nightmares returned. Not of murdering Klaus, oh no. It's been the same nightmare for eighty some-odd years. He goes to bed and it plays on repeat...

Walt remembers you can't escape the humidity in summer, and Klaus is there bitching about it in German the whole time. Everything, alive or dead, remains in a constant, moisturized state. It permeates your immediate reality in tandem with the heat, diffusing a stench of rot and decay. They slept, elevated in hammocks, sealed into a canvas cocoon. It blocks the light and some of the smell, same as it only blocks some of the bugs. Mild claustrophobia and stale air are a fair price for the minimal relief it offers.

Consciousness separates from the fog of sleep as Klaus shakes Walt's prone body. Walt stirs and realizes he's on the ground. This isn't good, snakes or bugs could find their way in. He reaches up to pop the button sealing the canvas. It's not there. Confused, he pushes forward with both hands. The canvas feels right, but it's as if someone had sewn it closed. Walt starts to panic. He grips at the canvas with his fingers, he pulls and tears and rips as hard as he can, thrashing his arms about, kicking his legs until the canvas rips open.

Klaus guides his hand. They find the zipper and peel it open. Cold air rushes in, raising goosebumps on his exposed flesh. Conical openings set high above his head trickle sunlight into a vast ship's hold. But why is he here? Walt looks around to find himself surrounded by hundreds, maybe thousands of bags. Some he recognized as hammocks, others were burlap sacks or cotton sheets. It dawns on him, these are body bags, which makes this a morgue ship.

"I'm alive!" Walt screams over and over again until he wakes up in a blind void.

But this time, there was no darkness, no waking abyss. Walter Maddox saw a soft glow in the distance, the first thing he'd seen in decades. It was beautiful to behold. He wasn't surprised to see Klaus standing there waiting, the same as he was the last time Walt saw him, immaculately dressed in his SS officer's uniform.

Hallo mein Freund, schön dich nach all den Jahren wiederzusehen. Klaus said, beckoning Walt to follow him. *Kommen. Wie, wie.*

Walt did as Klaus asked. The old soldier appreciated how wonderful the world had been to him for all the years he lived. Then Walt opened his eyes, let out one final breath, and followed Klaus into the light.

•

G ladys O'Connor made sure to put on her sexiest outfit tonight. After seeing Mrs. Coleman's boy, what a handsome young man he was, she couldn't wait. All the excitement at SummerHome got her horny like she was sixteen on prom night, all over again.

At eighty years of age, she concluded long ago sex kept you alive. The end results? She and Mike fucked as often as they could. They'd done so since meeting in college, right here in Fenton. They married on the day of JFK's assassination in 1963.

A few years before their nuptials, Gladys saw him sitting in the college dining lounge. She also saw the Cunningham girl staring at him.

What was her name? Gladys wondered. She couldn't remember. Gladys knew all about the Cunninghams, and the things people whispered about them and the other country folk outside of town.

"The Cunningham family tree is a trunk," she overheard her mother say once. Michael John O'Conner wasn't a filthy Cunningham, and the floozy cousin-fucker had no business looking at her Mike.

Gladys lived off-campus and drove to class. She gave her newfound love a ride to his dorm. He bragged about this new-fangled water bed he bought. Gladys Peabody rode Mike O'Conner's magic stick all night long and never once got seasick.

Yes, fucking kept the Grim Reaper away. With all the crazy bullshit going on in SummerHome lately, it turned up her libido. She found herself seeking the insertion of Mike's cock into one of her willing orifices far more often. He didn't mind. And it helped them both not think about what happened after that nice Dr. Al-Mahairi was killed in such a tragic accident.

Mike stepped out of the bedroom, awake from his nap to discover his wife all dressed up. A smile covered his face.

"What's the occasion baby?" He asked, still sitting in his reclining chair.

"Furniture delivery," Gladys winked, and Mike stood up.

"I wonder what kind of tip he'll get," Mike said.

"Screw him. I wonder what kind of tip *I'll* get," Gladys quipped. Mike wiggled his bushy eyebrows, stood, then the pair slipped off, hand in hand, into their bedroom.

They didn't see the cat watching from the shadows.

CHAPTER 12: Milk Cartons

The final rounds of the nurses rotated out on shift, and Richard "RJ" James, the custodian of SummerHome, punched out his second shift time card. It wasn't time for him to go home, though. He took care of Marion Webster on his time.

Marion's apartment, number 01, was the first apartment next to the employee break room, lockers, and time clock. He slipped out the door and let himself into Mrs. Webster's to perform his knightly duties in memory of his lost love. He hummed the melody of 'Elvira' as he walked into the apartment.

RJ didn't see the gray tabby cat snake into the apartment under his cowboy-booted feet. It retreated to a corner, obscured by the shadows.

The cat licked its whiskers, rested on its haunches, and watched.

•

A set of milk cartons, each displaying Roberta "Bobbie Be Good" Webster's smiling face, sat on top of a shelf commemorating the missing woman. The one item of Bobbie's recovered: a single, blood-stained boot, sat next to the wax paper carton. Framed, on the wall next to the bookshelf, rested a copy of Roberta's pride and joy, a demo CD of cover songs she made shortly before her disappearance. A half dozen MISSING posters, each featuring the same black and white image on the milk cartons, encircled the CD display. RJ made the sign of the cross as he passed the shrine to Bobbie Be Good.

"Hello RJ," Marion said.

"Hello, Marion," RJ replied, "what stinks so bad in here?"

"I think I tooted. I'm sorry. Did they say anything new about the doctor's accident? Because the news says the investigation into the cause is ongoing."

"They were outside in the lot all day. We had to park in the public lot, and that's caused some problems with the visitors."

"I'm sure it has. I hate to tell you this, RJ, but I poopied. Can you freshen me?"

"I sure can, Marion."

RJ always wore gloves and a mask when he wiped Marion Webster's ass. This was nothing new. It's a task he'd taken over for Bobbie since she disappeared all those years ago. Roberta Webster's disappearance during the Blizzard of '93 was one of the city's many unsolved mysteries and legends.

The Fenton rumor mill said she ran off with a rock star, some guy who sang at the bar. RJ remembered him and recalled he didn't like the long-haired dude. They found his car near her boot, but they never found him, and they never found Bobbie Be Good.

Ever since RJ took care of Marion, first at her trailer on the reservation, and now at SummerHome. The facility being his employer made the relationship more convenient to maintain. It was a perk RJ hoped for when he suggested Marion move here when the facility opened twenty years ago.

Now, as he neared retirement himself, RJ-who rented a room by the week at a local hotel and had done so for as long as three landlords could remember-amassed a private savings fortune, enough to put him up here when the time came.

Marion's crap smelled worse than normal tonight. He wondered what the kitchen was feeding her.

Beans, prune juice, and eggs, it had to be.

The stench crept up under RJ's mask and burned his sinuses, making his eyes water. Nausea and vertigo overcame him. RJ stepped back and blinked, pursing his lips under the protective mask.

"Marion, what in the achy-breaky double-hockey sticks did you eat in that cafeteria today?" RJ asked the old woman, lisping his words. He left his dentures home, and forgot them again, "Marion, you hear me?"

She didn't answer. A moment ago, she was all Chatty Cathy about the Doctor's car accident, and now she's not talking at all.

He poked her exposed ass cheek.

She didn't move.

"Marion?" RJ repeated, each word he spoke engulfed more of the wretched smell of decay and rot. He tasted it on his lips and tongue. It brought bile up in his esophagus, burning his throat. He soon learned the stench brought friends.

RJ didn't want to believe his eyes when he saw the first tentacle slither out of Marion's 90-year-old asshole. Initially, he thought she might be popping out another turd.

But turds don't wiggle.

The tentacle inched its way out. Gray, with a silvery sheen, a thin layer of viscous mucus lubricated the appendage. Miniature suction cups pulsated, with rows of pinprick teeth clenched around the circumference of each pad. It tested the air, making an exploratory gesture, before slapping onto Marion's butt cheek. Another soon followed, as did a few dozen more pseudopods. Within moments, a flower of the tendrils bloomed out from Marion's rectum, covering the woman's behind.

"Muh-muh-muh Marion? We need to call the nurse. You got a tapeworm or something!" RJ blurted out before his stomach evacuated its contents. The man's toothless mouth opened wide.

With the force of a firehose, he projectile vomited, the stream splashing off of Marion's prone, tentacle-covered backside. Chunks of pizza crust and masticated mystery meat filled the puree.

A back blast of spew erupted, covering everything within reach of RJ with puke. The steaming, vile mixture coated the floor and dripped from the ceiling.

RJ stood, bent over at the waist, his hands on his thighs. He took deep breaths as his diaphragm continued to spasm. Mucus bubbled up around his nostrils before dripping from his nose. The solid chunks of upchuck slid down his arms and legs, and off his neck.

What's happening? RJ couldn't grasp this, any of it. He closed his eyes, wishing away what he knew must be a hallucination. *Did tapeworms look like that? How can this be real? Was there eggs in the calamari from lunch and now she had baby octopuses growing in her guts?* The thoughts raced through his head at lightspeed, the words running into each other as he tried to process all this.

The sound of something heavy and plastic flopping into a puddle of barf broke RJ from his shock. He opened his eyes. A single rubber boot, an LL Bean duck boot, lay on the floor between him and Marion's squid-infested ass.

"Bobbie?" RJ said. He trembled. The boot was the same style as Bobbie Webster wore so many years ago. *How?* RJ wondered, *where did it come from?* He looked up to Marion's prone body on the bed and RJ's trembling turned into a full-on terror attack.

The tentacles growing out of Marion's ass were no longer docile. They danced about, tasting the air and feeling for something, anything to grab on to.

Things like RJ.

A tentacle wrapped around RJ's neck and squeezed. He threw his hands up, trying to pull it off. The appendage grew tighter and pulled him toward Marion. He choked and spit as he fought, his booted feet slipping in the ejecta.

If he won the battle to stay vertical, RJ might've

gotten away, if he could escape the tendril's grip. He might have, too, after falling, but a dozen more tentacles grabbed hold of him, each a steel vice. The tiny teeth on the tentacle suction cups bit into his flesh, slicing through the skin as the pseudopods slithered and coiled. Blood oozed out between the coils.

RJ could tell the tentacles were lifting him off the ground, he felt his feet dangling in the air. He kicked and thrashed, but the tentacles held him in a firm grip.

The tentacles retracted.

RJ's face slammed into Marion's bony backside. The curved ischium bones surrounding the coccyx at her tail bone shattered on impact, turning into jagged shards. As the tentacles pulled his head into the old woman's ass, these bits of shrapnel pierced through RJ's eyes and nasal cavity, entering his brain and temporal lobe, lobotomizing him.

In the last microseconds of his life, Richard James finally found peace after nearly thirty years of searching for his lost love.

•

T*he gray tabby cat stepped out of the shadows. It feasted on the ghostly squid as the tentacles dissolved and disappeared. Then it, too, faded into the darkness.*

·

The morning CNA at SummerHome, a new employee named Brenda, opened Marion Webster's door to find more than she anticipated. Blood and vomit covered the floor, but the display on Mrs. Webster's bed stopped her in place.

"What the fuck?" The nursing assistant screamed.

Marion Webster's prone body laid on her bed, dead, with the equally dead Richard James' head buried in her ass up to his shoulders. The whole scene resembled a weird arthouse painting of a centaur made from two humans.

No tentacles, no rubber boot.

No cat.

Only the amalgamated remains of Marion Webster and Richard James remained. Well, all of this plus Brenda DuBois screaming madly.

Death is a common occurrence at any nursing aid facility. If only she discovered a resident's dead body during her morning rounds, like Dawn, the aid assigned to Walter Maddox who passed away in his sleep over the same night. This she could have handled.

But fucked up shit like this?

Ms. DuBois quit her job at SummerHome after giving her statement to the police. She ignored the calls from New York City on her caller ID, believing they were from telemarketers and not realizing they were from persons interested in giving her financial restitution for talking to them about her experience. When she finally listened to the voice mails, a few days later when the power returned, it was too late. By then, the news informed her walking out on this job may have saved both her privacy and her life.

Part Two

Para-Hunters

CHAPTER 13: The Trial of Isle Magee

Isle Magee, County Antrim, Ireland
Three hundred years ago...

Morning dawned a new day. Trapped under a deep fog, the green, rolling hills of Ireland flowed to the sea. Along the way, fields and farm plots gave way to settlements. The land then scattered into smaller islands dotting the coastline.

By midday, the sun burned away the fog hanging over the coastal village where half the residents farmed and the other half fished. Normally, the residents would be found bustling about, tending to their chores.

But on this day no one tilled the fields or cast nets.

Instead, chaos and screaming filled a courthouse. Within the walls of the public forum, a mob of spectators, spilling out into the streets and town square, hurled curses and prayers at eight defendants on trial.

"Burn the witches!"

"Hang them! Hang them!"

"Harlots of Satan!"

"Burn them!"

The defendants, all women, wore skirts and petticoats with bonnets, indicative of ladies in early Eighteenth-Century Ireland. Standing, their hands were bound and their feet shackled. They turned their heads down, refusing to look at their accusers.

All but one.

Young, comely, and barely a woman, with striking red hair and emerald green eyes, she showed no fear or shame for her predicament. She appeared nonchalant about the whole affair, as if it were a petty nuisance to be disregarded on a whim.

The banging of a gavel, followed by a man crying desperately for order in the court, proved her bravado to be in vain.

"Order! We shall have order! *SILENCE, YOU CRETINS!*" A foppish man in a black robe and white wig declared. His face was powdered a matching white, and his jowls were highlighted with rose dust.

A ball of mud struck the Judge in the cheek. This didn't amuse him. He singled out a random attendee and pointed a finger at him. He didn't care if it was the person who threw the mud or not.

"Bailiff! Arrest that man for contempt of court. He can spend a night in the stocks!"

A bailiff grabbed the man. He protested until a blow to his head from the bailiff's balled fist knocked the man unconscious. The Judge continued to strike his gavel on the podium in front of his bench.

This finally caught the attention of the unruly. They settled down to whispers and mumbles until those trickled away to silence.

"Bring forward the accused!" The Judge commanded. The Sheriff grabbed the red-headed woman by a shoulder and dragged her in her chained feet to the floor in front of the Judge. She did not protest.

"Mary Brigit Dunbar, it is the verdict of this court to sentence ye to death by hanging for the crime of witchcraft. For being in league with Satan. For-"

"I didn't find Satan under the mound, did I, ladies?" Mary interrupted the judge. She blew a kiss to the bench and the other women giggled. The brazen acts by the accused mortified the crowd into whispers of awe.

"SILENCE! BE SILENT WITH YOUR LIES!" The Judge commanded, his voice booming. He made eye contact with the Sheriff. The officer slapped the woman in the face with a gloved hand. The smack was sharp and cracked, resonating throughout the courthouse.

A stream of blood trickled out from her lip. She

smiled in response, with a mischievous grin. It appeared as if she enjoyed the punishing blow.

She did.

"For," he continued with the charges, "seducing the good women of Isle Magee into servitude to Lucifer-" Mary Dunbar broke out in hysterical laughter. The other accused women followed suit and they drowned out the Judge. The Sheriff punched her in the face with his fist. A splash of blood burst from her mouth.

The laughter faded. A hush fell across those in attendance.

"What could ye find humorous in the sentencing of thy death?" The Judge inquired, "please indulge me, Goody Dunbar."

"Feck, ye'll learn soon enough. Blood is reaped and sewn, is it not sisters?" She cast a wicked grin as spoke, her words ever defiant.

"*Baintear agus fuaitear an fhuil!*" The accused chanted in chorus. The attendees gasped in shock, fearful they heard the incantation of a witch's spell.

They had.

"There'll be no witchery here, in this place of law. SILENCE THEM!" The Judge ordered and banged his gavel into the podium. Bailiffs and guards set to the task of covering the mouths of the accused. Mary didn't fight back when the Sheriff stuffed a wadded ball of cloth into her mouth.

She liked it.

"Ye are to be taken to the Isle Magee monastery on the morrow," he pointed at Mary with a shaking hand, "and hung until dead in the courtyard! May God have mercy on thy souls. Take these wretches away!" The Judge waved his hand and the bailiffs, with the Sheriff at their lead, led the accused away.

A sea of people stood outside of the courthouse, three times as large as those with prime seating. They spread throughout the village square, waiting for the results of the trial. A burst of commotion grew in volume as word of the verdict spread like a wildfire.

Preceded by deputies of the court, the guilty marched into the street. The jail was across town, and the villagers opened a parade way for the women to march down. With Mary Dunbar, at the lead, the Sheriff and bailiffs escorted the women to their temporary lodging.

It became a gauntlet.

The townsfolk first threw vegetables and cursed the women for their transgressions against God. This evolved. First, into mud, and then stones and rocks. A few brave souls came forward and physically assaulted the women as they passed by, punching or kicking them.

The women never cried out. They never winced. They never made so much as eye contact with any of their assaulters. With the exception of Mary, the others continued to stare down at the muddy street beneath their feet. It was as if they were immune to the hazing.

But it was at the end of their passion while waiting at the door of the jail, where the worst of it was dealt to young Mary Brigit Dunbar herself. The Sheriff halted the procession and fumbled with his keys to open the jail's door.

A goodwife, wrinkled and aged, stepped out of the crowd. She grasped a long, rusted, iron nail in her hand.

"Mum?" Mary Dunbar said, recognizing the woman. The woman lunged at Mary, "Mum, it's me, Mary Brigit, your daughter, what are you doing?"

"Yer not me child! No child of mine be in league with the Divil! Ye be a changeling!" The haggard woman screamed.

"No, Mum! No!"

The woman thrust the nail at Mary's throat. The Sheriff deflected the blow from ripping Mary's neck open. It didn't, however, prevent the point from raking up her face, and poking into the captive girl's eye.

Mary Brigit Dunbar screamed in agony for the first time since the trial began.

The old woman lost her grip and the spike tumbled into the mud. Blood and fluid squirted out of Mary's eye. A splash of it landed on the Sheriff's face, covering his mouth and nose. He licked the mixture on his lips and spit it out, before wiping his face with his gloved hand. It created stripes of crimson, giving the Sheriff a horrifying visage.

The Sheriff drove the heel of his boot into the old woman's neck before she could stand.

"Mum! No! Not my Mum! She be innocent! No!" Mary screeched in horror. The Sheriff ignored her pleas. The girl who remained so stoic and defiant throughout the trial, crumbled.

"Ignorance is not innocence," the Sheriff declared, "this is what happens to vigilantes!" He shifted his weight onto her neck, crushing her windpipe. The old woman thrashed about in the mud, punching the Sheriff's leg. He didn't move until she stopped convulsing. She vomited blood on his boot in her death throes. He wiped it off on her dress.

The crowd scattered. No one wanted to face the Sheriff's wrath. His reputation as a cold, unforgiving soul preceded him; and this exhibition of it surprised no one.

"Bind her wound, we won't let her escape the noose that easily!"

Mary wept as a bailiff covered her wound with a swatch of cloth, and tied it around her head. Her head throbbed in agony, and the pressure of the bandage helped lessen the pain. The Sheriff pushed her inside her cell. The other accused soon followed.

"*Blood will be reaped, I promise you that! Blood will be reaped, and sewn! Baintear agus fuaitear an fhuil!*" Mary cursed as the door to the jail closed.

"We'll see about that on the 'morrow," the Sheriff said as he locked the door. Inside, the witches of Isle Magee awaited their execution at the tolling of the morning bell.

•

Taken from "INFAMOUS WITCHES VOLUME II, THE 18TH CENTURY" by Theodore Buffett © 1997. Currently out of print:

Dubbed by some as the Salem of Ireland, the Island Magee Witch Trials in County Antrim were the last known witch trials in Ireland. The trial is alleged to have occurred during the spring of 1711. The historical record shows no indication executions were carried out. In 1712, the population of Isle Magee and nearby parts of County Antrim were devastated by an unknown epidemic and left uninhabited for a decade. All written files regarding this event were lost to fire during the Irish Civil War some 150 years later, in 1922. There are/were no further records of the women involved.

CHAPTER 14: Omens

Sean sat on the loading dock of the Donahue's Furniture warehouse waiting for the Ashley driver to back his truck up to the loading bay. He pulled in half an hour ago, and the truck remained in place since. It would take Sean roughly half an hour to unload the truck, all of it light-weight, premade pieces of furniture. Chairs, dining room tables, sofas, and so forth. But no couches.

Don't call them couches, fucking Goldbergs sells couches. Donahue's Furniture sells goddamned sofas. Gorman would say whenever a new furniture handler in the warehouse made the mistake of using a misnomer in his presence.

Knowing his luck, SummerHome would call the minute the truck backed in, and then Sean would be the asshole for taking a personal call and holding the driver up. His mother's condition concerned Sean. He still owned a bucket full of regret for committing-*no, that's not the word, it sounds like she's been sent to a mental asylum. The better word is 'moving', yes*-moving defined the action he and Meghan performed when they put Mom in the home.

Put. They *'put'* her there. Using the word within this parlance disgusted him. He couldn't escape it. Anything he said to himself to justify it gave Sean anxiety. He visited his mother there every day after work, and now the idea of going to a counseling session over his mother's dementia seemed silly to him. But Meghan decided for him.

And wouldn't it be the bad luck of the Irish for the place to be haunted?

Of course, it would. With JRR Tolkien villains. It brings us presents, me Precious!

He broke his gaze from the truck and looked up to check the time. The giant, white circle of a clock hanging above the bay doors read one thirty-five. Except for the occasional sofa sleeper, the Ashley truck could be unloaded in no time. The problem at hand considered the current time. Sean's break came at two o'clock, and the window of opportunity to get the truck unloaded before this time started ticking down five minutes beforehand.

Sean got antsy, and jumped off the bay into the

parking lot. He lit a cigarette, took a long drag, and walked to the big eighteen-wheeler, fifty yards away. The semi, a Big Mack, pulled a fifty-three-foot-long trailer decorated with the black and orange Ashley logo. Four drags later, Sean reached the cab. The diesel engine idled, spewing exhaust out.

He heard the music as he neared the cab. Classic rock guitars, the riffs in The Dark's song Full Balloon, blared through the cab's speakers. Sean slapped his hand on the cab door.

"Hey man, you pulling in anytime soon?" The chorus to the song answered Sean.

Drink the Kool-Aid! Drink the Kool-Aid! And the truck continued to hum along as it idled. But no one answered.

Did he take a nap in his sleeper? Sean wondered. He slapped the door again, this time harder.

"Hey man, everything alright in there? Anyone home?" He shouted, louder.

Aside from the idling engine and music, nothing else made any noise. Sean took another long drag off the cigarette. The mid-afternoon summer sun beat down on the parking lot and reflected off the trailer. Standing in the center of a sea of black, sweat leaked off Sean's mop of reddish-brown hair and down his face, stinging his eyes.

"Motherfucker," he whispered, pulled a bandana out

of his back pocket, and dried his face of sweat. He decided to give the trucker one last knock before heading back into the warehouse. The song ended and Sean saw his opportunity.

"Hey man, you awake?" This time, Sean slapped the door so hard it popped open.

A torrent of orange arterial blood poured off of the cab's floor and out the door. Sean jumped back on reflex, and in good measure. Without the door to hold him up, the truck driver listed and succumbed to the power of gravity. He moaned as he fell, and landed on his side in the puddle of his blood, splashing Sean's jeans.

"Holy shit! What the fuck happened?" Sean didn't know the driver, the Ashley guys were always someone different, their fleet of drivers being as large as it is. He didn't wear a name badge on his work shirt, either.

"My... my leg, it's cut open. My shifter..." the man managed to say before passing out. And Sean saw it. The driver wore shorts. A long, thin line of crimson traced up his right leg. Sean saw the driver clutching a cell phone in his bloodied hands, but the screen smashed when he landed on the blacktop.

What do I do? What do I fucking do? Sean thought, the words racing through his head at lightspeed. And then he figured it out. There wouldn't be time to run into the warehouse and call Gorman on the intercom. He needed to act now or this guy would bleed out.

Sean ripped his belt off and wrapped it around the driver's leg. Then he pulled it tight as possible, hopefully cutting off the circulation and stopping the blood flow.

Please God, let this work! Sean silently prayed.

The driver grabbed Sean by his neck, coagulating blood smearing every place in the process. For a man bleeding to death, he possessed the strength of a bowl-winning offensive line. Sean choked and gagged as the dying man pulled Sean down onto the ground next to him. The air around the driver's face shimmered, distorting his features, creating ever-shifting, bulbous outgrowths in the flesh.

Do ye see this blood? The driver said, his voice garbled and effeminate with a slight Gaelic brogue, *There'll be more than ye can ever imagine, it will pour down like runoff snow on a mountain in spring, it will be everywhere, Sean Michael Spencer, and it will drown ye and all ye love! Ye can stop it! Drive an iron spike through 'er heart with a shillelagh!*

"How? How do you know my name?" Sean struggled to speak.

Thrice times thrice, she comes for thee. Witchwood and iron! Witchwood and iron!

The driver released Sean from his grip. Spence scurried back on his ass, doing a reverse crab walk, putting as much distance as he could between himself and the driver.

The blood is reaped and sewn, Sean Michael. Witchwood and iron! Witchwood and iron!

"Spence! Are you okay!" Sean heard Gorman shouting from across the parking lot. Sean waved his hands in the air, motioning the warehouse manager to join him. Though short in stature, Gorman ran down in record time. He didn't need to ask Spence what happened. He saw it. Without hesitation, he called 911 on his cell phone. The operator answered and Gorman went to business.

"Yes, this is Chris Gorman, warehouse manager at Donahue's. We've got a truck driver out here bleeding to death, looks like he cut his leg open on something in his cab. We need a fucking ambulance for this guy and yesterday. We're in the back parking lot of the warehouse."

Sean sighed in relief.

"You slipped in his blood I see. What a mess. I saw him fall out of the trailer on the remote cameras in the office, so I knew something was going on. You put that tourniquet on him, Spence?"

"I sure did."

"Well, you might have saved his life doing so. Good job man. You can take the rest of the day off, with pay.

Don't punch out, I'll take care of it for you. Go home and get cleaned up."

"Thanks, Gorman. Let me know how this guy makes out." Sean said and walked across the parking lot, straight to his car. The drive home would allow Sean Spencer to call his sister at her work, for once. The words of the trucker resonated in his head as he walked away.

The blood is reaped and sewn! Witchwood and iron! Witchwood and iron!

•

The Lilac Grove Hair salon's location in the center of downtown Fenton gave its occupants a twisted view of the small city's busy main street. A large storefront window allowed the public to peer in and watch the hair stylists at work. The reflection from the interior of the salon created ghost images the passers-by drifted through as they walked past. They reminded Meghan of her dreams the night before.

The cell phone tone for her brother, Sean, roared through the hair salon, snapping her from her trance. She made Ozzy Osbourne's Over the Mountain, his favorite song, into his personalized ringtone, figuring he'd appreciate the sentiment. Which he did. But she never expected to hear it at two-thirty in the afternoon, a full ninety minutes before her brother got out of work.

Something must have happened, she resolved, retrieved her phone from her purse, visually verified it was her brother, and answered the call.

"Am I going insane?" Sean asked his sister, without so much as saying hello.

"What, no hello?" She said as she suppressed the urge to tell him to join the club, "no, hey sis, how are you doing? You just go into the meat of the conversation, okay then. To answer your question, I would have to ask another question."

"Like what?"

"Going? You've been a couple of ingredients shy of a full banana fudge sundae ever since I've known you, big brother."

"Oh, fuck you, Meghan," he cursed her out, then he told her what happened at work with the truck driver, leaving out the things Sean didn't believe. She, too, held back on telling him about her dream.

Memory?

"So, to answer your earlier question, no, I don't think you're insane. But I do think maybe you should see a doctor because it sounds like he smacked your head on the asphalt."

"He didn't, though. This is all fucked up. What does

"witchwood and iron' or *'blood is reaped and sewn'* mean about anything, for fuck's sake."

"Excuse me?" the phrases from her dreams, coming out of her brother's mouth, caught her off guard. How could he know, "what did you say?"

"Witchwo-"

"No, the other thing?"

"Blood is reaped and sewn?"

"Where did you hear that?"

"The trucker I saved today. He said it when he was ranting, delirious from blood loss. Why, have you heard it before?"

"No," Meghan lied, shrugging her shoulders, "I thought you said something else. Did you get enough sleep last night, I mean, with everything going on with Mom and all?" Meg was skilled at changing subjects, and her brother fell for it every time.

"I got plenty of sleep."

"Then I don't know. Is there anything else you care to share?"

"Nope, that's it. Okay, I'm almost to Moms. I'll see you soon."

Meghan hung the call up with her brother. She stared out the window of the salon and watched a produce truck with a giant, smiling anthropomorphic banana on the side drive through her reflection. She slid her phone into her purse and went back to work, thinking of black butterflies, falling rain, and the words. They all came back to haunt her from the dream world.

Blood is reaped and sewn.

CHAPTER 15: Viral

Sean arrived early at SummerHome. Too shaken up to stay at the warehouse after what happened with the trucker, his heart stopped for a moment as he neared his mother's apartment. Walt's chess board was gone, and his apartment was open. Aids and orderlies were moving his belongings out.

Son of a bitch, Sean thought to himself, *he was a nice man.*

This time Sean knocked on his mother's door. She answered with a smile on her face.

"You're here early," she said. He embraced her and gave Maureen a giant bear hug.

"I've had another bad day and I don't want to talk about it."

"Fair enough," Maureen said.

Sean visited with his mother the rest of the day. The

two binged on old sitcoms, laughing whether the jokes asked for it, or not. They didn't talk about men bleeding to death or spirits possessing the body. Sean liked it better this way.

Before dinner, Maureen laid down for a nap. Sean stepped out of his Mom's apartment for a smoke when Gladys O'Connor shuffled by him in the hallway. He tried to keep a straight face. But try as he may, a smirk still broke the plane of his lips as she passed. Sean no longer saw the kind, blue-haired old lady.

My Precious! Instead, she would forever resemble Gollum to him. And this made him want to crack up. He chose to hide his mirth and did his best to retina straight face in front of the old woman.

"Hello, young man," Gladys said. "You're always smiling. I like to see that in younger people. Too many people are so serious all the time," Sean heard other words, instead, the hissing, falsetto tone of The Hobbit once known as Smeagol.

It caught us knocking bones, my precious and now it laughs at us!

"Why thank you, Mrs. O'Connor, right?" Sean asked.

"Yes, sweety, that's me!"

Me precious …

Sean continued on his way. But he knew someone, or something watched him. Part of him hoped little old

Gladys might be checking out his ass, wishing she was Priscilla again, and not Smeagol. But part of him smelled blood, and the Gollum voice in his head smelled it, too.

It brings us presents, witchwood, and iron. Blood is reaped, my precious, and blood... is... sewn... witchwood and iron!

A chill ran up his spine. Vertigo took over. He could barely stand up, let alone walk. He shook his head, hoping the bad thoughts would fly out of his mind.

They didn't.

A sense of dread flooded his body, giving him a new purpose. He needed to get outside and have a cigarette, smoke a joint, to do something to get the visions out of his head. He made a bee-line to an exit, power walking as fast as he could without running as he went. He reached the exit in record time. But when he opened the double doors, he stopped in horror, unable to move forward.

A translucent image formed before him. A wall of thick, viscous crimson crested before him, bubbling and frothing, threatening to flood the building.

Witchwood and iron. Blood is reaped and sewn! It wasn't Gladys' Gollum hazing him this time. He heard the same almost childlike voice he did from the trucker earlier in the day. Sean slammed the doors closed. He prayed no one was watching him have a nervous breakdown in the middle of SummerHome.

It's here and you can't escape it! The voice rang like thunder in Sean's head.

His phone buzzed in his pocket, breaking his focus on the voice.

And everything returned to normal.

He pulled the phone out of his pocket. The caller ID declared MEGHAN.

What the fuck is she calling me for? I'm here, Sean thought. He hesitated a moment longer, then answered.

"Hell-hello?"

"Hey, bonehead, it's your sister."

"Yes, I know. I'm at SummerHome. I was just seeing Mom and I'm going out to have a smoke."

"I'm on my way. How is she today?"

"She's fine, eating dinner right now."

"Good. Sorry, I couldn't make it in earlier, I had a booked day at the salon and it went over."

"That's fine. You can see her before she goes to bed, I'm sure."

"Yes, I can. Okie-Dokie, smokey. I'm gonna let you go, but I've got something I want you to watch. See ya in a flash," Meghan replied.

"Hold on. You know how Doctor Al-Mahairi died in the car accident the other night?"

"Yeah, what happened, did they find out he was

drunk or on drugs or something?"

"No. I overheard the aids talking today about how that creepy janitor who sings Elvira, and the lady he took care of, both died last night. And old man Walt, he died in his sleep, too."

"That's horrible! The old lady who told us the story at karaoke?" Meghan declared.

"Yeah, her. And the guy I was playing chess with. This place is starting to give me the creeps more and more. People are dying all the time."

"It's part of the deal here, big brother. They don't call it SummerHome for nothing, it's one of the last stops before eternity, you know?"

"Yeah, I know," Sean said goodbye and she hung up the phone. He put his phone back in his pocket and took a deep breath, then he opened the double doors of the exit. No blood awaited him this time, only the bright sunshine of the late summer evening.

Sean didn't see or hear the gray tabby cat with a white diamond on its chest, standing in the shadowed corner, lapping at something black on the darkened floor with earnestness.

A puddle of blood.

•

ean discovered Meghan sitting at his mother's dining table when he came back, watching videos on her cellphone. Her face was aghast in morbid curiosity.

"What's going on?" He asked.

"Look," Meghan motioned to her phone's screen. A cherub-faced young beat reporter from the local regional cable TV news network stood behind a news ticker declaring:

"HAUNTED RETIREMENT COMMUNITY? MURDERING POLTERGEISTS? IS A GHOST KILLING DOCTORS AND RESIDENTS AT SUMMERHOME?"

As it turned out, several videos of the recent incidents at SummerHome inhabited the vast internet archive. Less than twenty-four hours passed, three people died, and rumors of a ghost sighting by an unnamed resident-likely their mother-came to light. Any video of the news spectacle already owned six digits in views. And they were growing. Memes and links populated social media, making it trend in conversation and on social media, #hauntednursinghome.

"This! Look! I knew it!" Meghan threw an old photograph on the table, the photo from the hatbox she discovered in the attic, curled at its corners, spun on the table, "do you know who that is?"

"You? Mom's sleeping. Keep it down," Sean warned

his sister. His stress levels were through the roof and he wanted nothing more to do with any heavy thinking this day.

"No, it is not me. It's Mom! And I'll keep it down after you explain this lunacy to me. I knew I wasn't imagining it,"

"I never said you were. It looks like a picture of you as a kid with a butterfly floating in front of you. But what does this have to do with us and Mom?"

"Maybe that it is Mom and not me? But don't you find it odd? Like the photograph recreated itself in my dreams and came to life? And the smell of flowers and roses? Yesterday I asked her about this picture and the papers in the box before dinner. She was clueless. And then, on top of all this, she acted like it was nothing out of the ordinary to put stuff that should be in a file cabinet or safe in a random box."

"No, the only thing I find odd are the incidents themselves, and nothing to do with us. It's a coincidence, Meg."

"But why butterflies? Of all animals? And why the smell of a rose bush in a flower garden with no roses?"

"Fuck if I know. Your mind made it up cos you saw the picture? Someone was wearing rose perfume at your salon? Did Mom ever mention loving butterflies to you? 'Cause, she never did to me," Sean shrugged.

"But the flower garden in the backyard. It always had butterflies, all summer long. I know. I played in it all the time."

"Most flowery gardens do. You know, now that I think of it when she started to get sick," he pointed to his temple, "the first thing she gave up on was that garden. It's been rotting out there for a good five years now. Plus, I remember she hated roses. I brought some home for you at your graduation, remember? She flipped the fuck out."

"Oh, I know, preacher Sean, I am the choir director, if you recall. But look at all of this stuff!" Meghan retrieved another handful of papers from the box and slapped them on the table, "Look! Your birth certificate, and mine."

"Okay, and she stores that stuff in a hatbox? I don't know. She is losing her mind, after all, Megs."

"Look at you, all worried that I strong-armed you into putting her SummerHome-"

"Why do you have to bring that backup? Really? Okay, we did the right thing, I know we did. I'm sorry I said that."

"A lot of people keep saying they're sorry for things they've said, lately."

Meghan's phone rang. She dug it out of her purse and looked at the caller ID, revealing a number from New

York City, *555-697-7150*. It wasn't anyone in her contacts, so it must be a scam call or a bill collector. So, she passed it to voicemail.

"Anyone important?" Sean asked. Meghan shook her head, "as I was saying, she stopped caring about things a long time ago. And I don't know what this has to do with Mom and the crazy shit happening at SummerHome." The voice mail alert chimed on Meghan's phone.

Then Sean's phone rang.

He pulled it out of his pocket and saw a New York City number on the screen.

"Do I need to know a number in New York?"

"Let me see it," Meghan said. He showed her the phone. The number matched the one from moments before, "555-697-7150. Holy shit. Don't answer it."

"Why not? You think they want to sell us a fucking extended warranty on Mom's car?" Sean chuckled and didn't wait for Meghan to answer. He pressed the green icon on his phone, turned on the voice mail, and said, "Sean Spencer here. How can I help you?"

"Hi, Sean. This is JD Thompson from Ne-Pat, The Northeast branch of the Paranormal Assessment Team from the Sci-Fi Channel. You may have also seen our show *Para-Hunters*," Sean and his sister both knew of the long-running programs, they would watch them frequently with their Mom, "We'd like to talk to you about what's been happening at SummerHome."

Sean and Meghan stared at each other, astonishment decorating their faces.

"Hello? Are you there?" Sean sought Meghan's approval before answering. He shrugged his shoulders and raised his eyebrows. She nodded in response.

"Yes, we're here," Sean replied.

·

Meghan couldn't sleep, she tossed and turned on her bed. On the drive home, the same thought the same thing on repeat.

The Para-Hunters wanted to talk to their mother.

Wow.

Mom would be delighted, of course. She always loved the paranormal ghost hunting shows. She spent the hour mocking them, but this would be half the fun of watching it. We all knew ghosts didn't exist.

Right?

But now a respected ghost hunting team wants to talk to her about a potential haunting in her new home. And after the outburst with the doctor, she didn't know if talking to anyone outside of the family would be a good idea.

Sleeping, as it turned out, wasn't the choice to make.

•

Meghan's head throbs. She opens her eyes, and can't see out of them. She feels a binding on her head and feels something wet dripping down her cheek. With one eye, she sees a half dozen or so women standing next to posts in a courtyard. Their dress is anachronistic to her, and long petticoats cover their bodies. Simple wreaths of yellow and white flowers- daisies, chrysanthemums, black-eyed Susans, and dandelions- adorn their heads. Their hands are tied behind their backs, and each has a noose attached to their neck. The slack of the rope is tied to the post's top and each of the women stands on a log.

Meghan looks down to see she, too, stands on a log. She notes she is dressed the same as the others. Restrained the same as the others. She can feel the rope around her neck digging into her flesh.

A group of men stands before the women. She sees the sheriff and his deputies and recognizes them as the men who brought her to this place. A Judge, a Priest, and the latter's acolytes stand aside from them. The Sheriff steps up to Meghan. He pushes his tricorn cap back on *his brow and snarls at her.*

"Mary Brigit Dunbar," the Sheriff says, his words thick with the accent of a Gael, "ye and thee have been charged with crimes against the state. For being in league with dark and evil powers, for being concubines of the Divil, and for practicing witchcraft most foul and evil."

Meghan shakes her head.

"No, no, no!" Meghan screams back at the man, "You've got the wrong person! My name isn't Mary Brigit Dunbar, it's Meghan! Meghan Coleman!" Meghan hears her words and she does not recognize the voice.

"Listen to the lies coming from the whore's mouth!" The Priest says. And Meghan believes him, how can they be true if the voice saying them is not her own.

"Aye," the Sheriff nods, "all lies! Shut thy mouth, lest I shut it for thee, harlot of Satan!" He slaps her in the face, regardless. Meghan recoils from the sting of the strike.

"The witch's coven shall suffer before her eyes!" The Judge decrees. Meghan watches as the Sheriff's bailiffs approach each of the women. With smiles on their faces, the bailiffs kick the logs out from under each of the terrified women. All but Meghan.

The Sheriff hovers over her, leering at her. Holding her face with a gloved hand, he forces her to watch her coven hang.

"See thy evil's penance!" The Sheriff taunts her,

pointing at them with his free hand. The Judge and the Priest laugh at the suffering they have wrought.

The women kick, their bodies flailing in agony. They'd scream, but they are unable to as the women are hanging from their necks. Meghan, unable to turn her gaze away, watches as they suffer. Thrashing and choking, their tongues extend from their gaping mouths before they die, asphyxiated, one by one. Their bladders release as they expire, raining bloody piss on the ground beneath them.

"It is done," Meghan hears Mary say with her mouth, her tongue moving of its own volition.

"Aye, the deed 'tis done," the Sheriff pauses in his reply, "my love," then kisses Meghan/Mary on the lips. The bailiffs stare at the act in disbelief.

"So mote it be," Mary says in unison with the Sheriff. He draws his sword, a slim rapier, and in one fluid motion, slices the throats of both of the bailiffs. They each crumple to the ground, crimson bibs spreading down their chests.

Meghan, looking through Mary's eyes, sees the judge and priest. Terror grips them. The priest orders his acolytes to seize the sheriff. They run into his blade, instead. The Sheriff slices the rope and Meghan feels the noose fall limp on her-no, on Mary's- shoulders. She steps off the log onto the solid ground.

"Sheriff Magee! What is this blasphemy!" The Priest

screams. The Sheriff responds by pointing his rapier at the gentlemen. The Judge and the Priest run. The Sheriff catches them soon enough. Being portly men, the task of running is arduous. For the Sheriff, it's almost too easy as a choreographed dancer's well-practiced routine. He pounces upon them and runs each man through the heart as they pant and sweat, begging for their lives.

Meghan hears Mary laugh as her tormentors are singularly exterminated. It's a banshee's cackle, shaking the dreaming girl to the bone.

"The fondest memories are saved first, my pretty, oh, so pretty, young thing," Mary Dunbar says with Meghan's tongue. The words catch Meghan by surprise, for she knows the accused witch is speaking to her, and no one else. "Come to me, my love, blood shall be reaped and sewn. Baintear agus fuaitear an fhuil!"

The Sheriff finished with acts of murder, unbuckled his trousers and made haste in rejoining his betrothed. They embraced. Meghan watched the carnal act from inside Mary as the unholy matrimony between Sheriff Magee and his wife was consummated.

And she liked it.

•

L̲ike most of the night terrors before it, Meghan would forget the dream when she woke. But Biddy Magee wouldn't.

Biddy Magee never forgets.

CHAPTER 16: Media Circus

Both Sean and Meghan took the next day off from their respective employers and arrived at SummerHome early. The property shimmered with life. A carnival of lights from the vehicles of various news outlets lined the sidewalk areas around the facility. Luckily, none of them slipped into the restricted parking area for residents' families.

"I'm surprised there isn't a food truck," Meghan said when they exited the car.

"Tell me about it," Sean replied. The brother and sister knew the location of SummerHome's employee entrance. They opted for this route as opposed to dealing with the throng of cameras hovering about the front doors. Inside, the facility bustled with activity. The staff went about their business, tending to their wards at

SummerHome.

The residents, however, were more enthralled by the television news teams. They waited in line to film their ghost stories near the cafeteria. Much to their chagrin, Sean and Meghan were greeted by a smiling JD Thompson. The siblings knew who JD was, and after talking to him last night on the phone, they still couldn't believe this was real. He intercepted them as they passed by the shuffling residents. He introduced himself to the siblings and ushered them straight in for an interview.

"You're shorter and grayer than you look on TV," Meghan told him, enjoying her sarcasm more than she should.

"All the better to charm you with, my dear," Thompson replied, the stereotypical devilish grin smeared on his face. Meg wanted to gag. He was going to be one of them, the innocent flirter who wouldn't say no if the opportunity presented itself. She rolled her eyes.

He led them to a corner table where a gray-haired middle-aged couple sat. Meghan recognized them as the stars of Para-Hunters, the world-famous demonologist Ted Buffett and his psychic wife, Elaine. He sat down next to them and wasted no time in getting down to business.

"We'd like to set a couple of cameras up in your mother's apartment," JD Thompson said. Ted and Elaine

Buffett drank their coffee in silence. They always let JD do the talking, something they frequently regretted.

"And these are for?" Sean asked.

"They're standard with any remote we work on. The staff indicated your mother believed she saw a ghost in her room recently-"

"Our mother suffers from early-onset Alzheimer's," Meghan interrupted, "she thought she saw the ghost of my father."

"Yes, I'm aware of this. And we can probably rule her out because of that, but we can never be sure. The audience at home will want to know. It's good TV."

"Good TV? Is that what our mother is to you? Good fucking television?" Sean added. He couldn't believe his ears. This entire experience pissed him off.

"No, no. Not at all, Mr. Spencer. I used the wrong verbiage."

"You always use the wrong verbiage, Dad," a young sandy blonde-haired woman entered the cafeteria, "Hi, I'm Samantha Thompson, I'm JD's one and only child. Everyone calls me Sam. What my father is trying to say, and failing, is your family's battle is good for TV, it's educational. We'll present her with empathy, and the audience will bond with your family. No one will think you or she are crazy."

"I'm not sure about that," Meghan said, "we're

already a bit on the looney side."

"Ain't that the truth," Sean said and stifled a laugh.

"This isn't the time for jokes, or to be worrying about being embarrassed on television. Demons aren't funny, and they sure as shit don't give a flying fart if you get a little red-faced," Ted Buffett said. A somber, emotionless expression covered his face. His wife looked up from her coffee and clasped his shoulder.

"Don't scare the young ones, dear," Elaine said.

"They need to be scared," Ted replied.

"Scared of what?" Meghan asked. Sean held back from speaking when Samantha held her hands up.

"Okay, okay, okay, everyone, please," Sam said, "there is no proof of demons or any ghosts. We don't prejudge when coming to a haunting."

"There is no haunting. My mother has Alzheimer's and thought she saw her dead husband. Call the nurse who was on duty that day. She'll tell you the same thing." Sean's agitation grew with each word. His already short fuse found itself sizzling. Exhaustion from losing sleep.

And the nightmares.

My precious!

"We've called her and left messages," JD said, "she's not returning our calls."

"What does that tell you," Meghan spoke up, "she doesn't want to speak with you because there weren't any ghosts in our mother's bedroom."

"I'd be lying if I didn't say most of our cases have had logical, environmental, or medical explanations," Sam added.

"Most?" JD added, "more like all," and shrugged his shoulders. Ted shook his head and went back to his coffee.

"Well, yes," Sam continued, "all of our cases have been explained. That's what ghost hunters do. They prove a place isn't haunted."

Behind them, Elaine snorted and stirred her coffee with a spoon, making sure to clang it on the porcelain mug.

"Your show could've fooled us, we've watched Para-Hunters for years," Sean said.

"That's the magic of television," JD Thompson said, "everyone sees something different. They see what they want to see. In your case, the nurse claimed in her report she saw your mother's cat, and that startled her, but there was no ghost."

"See. It's all bullshit," Sean took the opportunity to set them straight, "she doesn't have a cat. We haven't had one in years."

"Are you sure?" Sam asked, tapping her pen on a clipboard.

"Yes, I'm sure," said Sean.

"According to the staff," Sam reviewed the notes on board, "it's always sleeping on her bed when they check on her at night."

"That's impossible," Meghan said, her mind recalling the euthanasia bill, "we put her cat down last year right before her stroke. Snuffy was its name. I named the cat when I was little."

"Yeah, no cat here, ever."

"See what I mean? There's lots of things to figure out here." JD interjected, "let's talk to your Mom, so we can get to the bottom of this and find out what she thinks, is that cool?" Sean and Meghan stared at each other in the eye for a brief moment. They turned in tandem to face the production team.

This guy could talk. But they could see through their facade of empathy. JD Thompson, his daughter, and their stars only cared about TV ratings.

Samantha's phone beeped. She glanced down at the screen.

"That was from SummerHome's managers," the producer said, "if we're going to film the segment in Webster's room, we need to go do it tonight before they move her stuff out."

"Webster? Her name was Marion," Meghan scowled as she corrected Samantha.

"Uh, yeah, this only proves our suspicions. So that'll

be a big no for talking with our Mom, too." Sean said, and Meghan nodded. The siblings left the table without looking back.

"You're a pair of fucking gems, good job on munging this one up." Sean and Meghan heard Elaine say as the doors closed behind them.

CHAPTER 17: Personal Darkness

The Para-Hunters entered Marion Webster's vacant apartment and set it up for production. The police had already taken what they needed. With no next of kin, SummerHome was set to donate her belongings to the Fenton Goodwill later in the day. Orderlies would be coming by in the next couple of hours to pack up the remainder of the deceased woman's long life.

This gave the production team a limited window. Samantha set up the cameras, lights, and mic booms as JD finished writing his notes. Ted and Elaine readied themselves, too. He scanned the apartment, looking for anything out of the ordinary. Elaine meditated as she always did before attempting to reach "the other side."

"Okay, I'm ready as I'll ever be for this one," the older woman said after breaking her catatonic, unblinking trance. Ted nodded and stood away from her, off-camera. JD stepped in front of the camera with Elaine by his side.

"SummerHome in Fenton, NY. On the outside, it resembles a typical retirement community. Inside, however, SummerHome could be the haunt of a murdering poltergeist." JD said as he and Elaine walked around the apartment. Sam followed them with the camera. "In one week, a trio of deaths has left the staff and residents numb. First, the head physician, Dr. Abrahaim Al-Mahairi tragically crashes his car. Then, in one night, two long-time residents of SummerHome pass away under mysterious circumstances. Add to this rumors of other ghostly apparitions making appearances within these sterile halls and you will ask yourself, 'Is SummerHome the lair of a deadly paranormal entity? And if so, why, who is it, and how do we exercise it from the premises?' Well, the NEPAT team is here to answer all of these questions for you. Join us now, why don't you, for one of the scariest investigations to date as we enter the haunted nursing home on this episode of Para-Hunters! CUT!" JD declared, and Sam turned off the camera.

"Okay, let's get Elaine set up for her psychic investigation scene," Sam said. Upon entering a haunt, Elaine would attempt to visualize the events of the night before, often repeating what was written in the police report. It was a highlight of the show, one of its best-rated segments for the hour. Samantha knew, like a band playing live, if the opener didn't grab the audience, they weren't likely to stick around for the rest.

"I don't know, I feel off today like something isn't right," Elaine said.

"Like what?" JD asked.

"This place, it's unsettling. I don't like it, not one bit."

"Alright, let's get this done then and call it a day."

"Yes, please," Elaine said and sat at the dinner table and crossed her arms. She closed her eyes and Sam turned the camera back on. The lights flooded the dining room and cast black shadows behind the woman.

Elaine bowed her head. After a few moments, the others could hear her talking in tongues, a common occurrence when they happened upon what they would call a true haunting. What wasn't common was Elaine sitting straight up in her chair, with her eyes bugged out, screaming bloody murder. Blood dripped down her right cheek from an invisible wound. Then she collapsed on the table convulsing. JD and Ted ran to her. Sam kept the video going, staring at the screen.

"Turn the fucking camera off, Sam!" Ted ordered her. Either she ignored him or was too much in shock to react, Ted didn't care. She kept staring through the video screen. "I said turn the fucking thing off before I throw it at the wall," he threatened. The producer turned it off and stepped away from the camera, trembling.

•

Unlike the bulk of the herd of charlatans on television, those sideshow carnies pretending to be psychic mediums, Elaine Buffett was the real deal. At least she believed so, how else could anyone explain what she experiences in these circumstances? But she felt certain Houdini would have authenticated her if she lived a century before.

Sitting at the table, crossing her hands on its

surface, Elaine prepared to go to her *personal darkness*, the place she went when looking at the other side. She learned this trick when she was a girl becoming a young woman; a time when the changes in her body brought more than breasts, pubic hair, growth spurts, and periods.

Elaine saw her first ghost quite by accident, shortly after her twelfth birthday when she was still Elaine Toth. During a family outing to a local beach, while sunning herself, Elaine fell into a semi-meditative state.

The girl entered her *personal darkness* for the first time. Her mind was somewhere between the beach and the netherworld of the spirit, a dream world where all we've ever been, and ever will be, simply *is*. This included the spiritual imprints of the recently dead.

Devoid of color, Elaine saw a world resembling a black and white television being recorded on an analog video camera. Streaks and lines floated in her now color-blind vision, warping her perceptions, with each line and bubble showing her a glimpse of the beach during all states in time. Dazed at first, and fascinated by what she was seeing, she almost missed seeing him on the beach. The figure of a young boy kneeling in the surf along the ocean.

At first, Elaine believed him to be another child playing in the water. But he didn't move. He stayed there, unattended, for far longer than a child should be left alone. Elaine wondered where his parents or guardians were.

When he turned and faced her, she saw his bloated facial features. He pointed to a rocky pier with a pale arm and crooked fingers. Then she noticed the waves didn't break around his body, they passed through him, and Elaine knew the answer. Instinct told her what she was observing: the ghost of a dead boy.

It didn't startle or scare her. Instead, her curiosity grew as she continued to observe. Her mother called her, shining a light on Elaine's *personal darkness*, and Elaine slipped out from the semi-lucid state.

The spirit of the dead boy washed away with the tide as the girl's vision regained its grip on reality. Elaine and her family packed up their beach chairs and towels. Near the breaking pier by the parking lot, Elaine noticed a poster tacked to a telephone pole.

'MISSING,' it declared, with a picture of the ghostly boy she saw in the water. Elaine pointed to the pier.

"What's this all about?" She recalled her mother asking her.

"This boy is in the rocks down there," Elaine told her.

"How do you know this?" Her mother questioned.

"I just do, it makes the most logical sense," she continued to lie. Elaine kept her source a secret and never told her parents while they were alive, or dead. A bright girl known for her assertiveness, Elaine knew what happened to kids in 1960s America who claimed to see things. She didn't much care for ice picks or lobotomies.

To prove her point, Elaine insisted her mother and father follow her to the pier. With the low tide, they could see through the cragged rocks. At the base of the stones, partially hidden in a bed of seagrass, was the missing boy. Shocked by the discovery, Elaine continued her ruse, telling everyone it was a lucky guess.

Everyone except for her sweetheart, Teddy Buffett. She bled her heart out to him about her visions. He didn't mock her, judge her, or call her crazy. A devout Catholic, Teddy saw Elaine as being blessed with a gift from God.

The pair married as soon as they both graduated from college, Elaine with a degree in psychology and Ted with one in television and communications. After her parents passed, Elaine presented an idea to Ted, to follow in the footsteps of those carnies, the Warrens, with one exception:

Elaine wasn't full of shit.

Twenty years later, their vision is still drawing numbers. Their syndicated television show, the Para-Hunters, has been going strong for the entire time, overcoming network changes and the ever-changing viewer watching habits. Keeping up with the times, their YouTube channel has two and half million followers. Elaine knew they may not have movies like the Warrens, but the Para-Hunters didn't need a movie.

Elaine shifted in her chair and stared at the camera in Samantha's hands. The lens became her focal point. Her eyes fluttered, then closed, and her consciousness slipped into the black and white elsewhere of her *personal darkness.*

•

Behind the lids of her closed eyes, Elaine observed the apartment as it was, and as it ever will be. The color pallet matched a photo negative of the real world. The furniture flickered and shifted in a constant pattern, and a smokey haze filled the rooms.

Both were commonplace and told Elaine a bit about the location. The former amalgamated the furnishings to inhabit the apartment, while the latter indicated at some point the building would burn down.

Elaine was alone in the room. Samantha and JD and Ted were still with her, each a flickering reflection of themselves in Elaine's paralogical nether-realm. What she expected to see, the ghosts of Marion Webster and Richard James, wasn't here. They were nowhere to be found.

A gray tabby with a brilliant white diamond on its chest jumped up on the table, startling Elaine and almost breaking her out of her state. It did what cats do, purring and rubbing up against Elaine's arms and upper body. When a typical house cat practices this behavior, it releases oxytocin, in humans. It's a bonding and love secretion responsible for the motherly feeling one experiences during childbirth. It's a survival mechanism for cats.

But this wasn't a typical house cat.

Its touch released a decidedly different pair of hormones, adrenaline, and cortisol. The cocktail coursed through Elaine's bloodstream. It first caused a pit to form in her stomach before anxiety set in and her limbs trembled.

It looked Elaine in the eyes. She looked back.

"Look at ye, a hedge witch peeking into the twilight where ye don't belong," the cat said, its words masculine with a Gaelic brogue, "since ye be here, I may as well entertain ye. There be things in the twilight world, terrible things, lassie. Things worse than the dead moving on. Here, let me show ye. Baintear agus fuaitear an fhuil."

The apartment peels away and disintegrates into

pixelated specks. In the mist of clouds an opaque, green eye stands guard, observing in a silent vigil.

"There be demons in the snows 'round here," the cat says, *"and things much older under the mound."*

The snow melts, revealing a landscape of luscious, rolling hills. The eye transforms into a blazing midsummer sun. At the base of a cairn, Elaine sees a sun-bleached skull with a wreath of dried flowers resting atop it. It welcomes observers with a displaced jaw. Behind the grinning effigy, Elaine notices a shimmering doorway at the base of a small hill.

"Under the mound, behind this door, lives things. Dark things more vile than the Divil himself, with secrets older than the God of Abraham. Baintear agus fuaitear an fhuil!"

A swarm of chaotic energy bursts out from the opening in the mound. Elaine sees color in her personal darkness. It's in shades of red ranging from pink to crimson and maroon. She can't stop staring at the colors. The patterns of red swirl in the air and form a body and face. It's a familiar face, one she has seen before, but Elaine can't place it. Frustration takes over. She hears herself screaming but she can't do anything to stop it.

The cat strikes at Elaine, swiping her face with its ethereal claws. Her soul feels the nails scraping down her face, across her eye. The blow stings, drawing blood, and she throws her hand up to cover her eye.

"No matter what ye do, hedgewitch, the blood shall be reaped and sewn, I promise ye that!" The cat says, turns its head, and stares at the camera.

Into the camera.

The camera stares back and Samantha sees it, too.

It mews one last time.

"Baintear agus fuaitear an fhuil!"

•

Samantha watched the ghostly cat through the camera. She heard it speak to her, and she listened to the things it said. She saw the things it revealed. And she froze in fear.

Blood is reaped and sewn. The words echoed in her brain on repeat.

"I said turn the fucking thing off before I throw it at the wall!" Ted screamed at her, breaking her from her catatonia, still trying to process what she saw. She switched off the camera and saw Elaine shaking and crying, sitting at the table still, Ted consoling her. Sam didn't know if she wanted to turn it back on ever again.

A few tense minutes of silence and sniffling from Elaine lasted until JD came to Sam's side.

"What happened?" He asked.

"I froze, I can't say why," Sam lied then asked, "is Elaine okay?"

"I think so," Ted said, "why would you record her in such a state? That's not right."

"Sorry, Ted, I was kinda freaking out, too."

"Yeah, well, we're done here for the day, I think."

"Stop it, Teddy, It's fine, she didn't do anything wrong," Elaine interjected, "but I do agree, I don't want to spend any more time here than I have to. I'll tell you this much, this place isn't haunted," Elaine said.

"It isn't?" JD said, his face betraying his disappointment and surprise at the revelation.

"Something far more evil has its grip on these grounds."

"It's demonic?" Ted asked his wife. She shook her head no.

"Then what is it?" JD continued the questioning.

"I don't know. And that's what scares the living shit out of me."

CHAPTER 18: My Precious

Mike O'Connor stared at his wife and drooled in anticipation. Gladys's blonde wig and white dress recalled Marilyn Monroe in the Seven Year Itch. She wore a similar dress on her wedding day. She sure felt like a sexy bombshell in the outfit.

"Happy birthday to you. Happy birthday to you. Happy birthday Mr. President," Gladys sang as Mike stepped into their bedroom. He wore a dapper suit, pressed. His hair teased back. She turned an oscillating fan on. A powerful wind blew her dress and hair, making a mess of the wig. She fought a losing battle to keep it straight on her head. He knew it was time to get busy.

"Ask not what your President can do for you, ask what you can do for your President," he said, and dropped his pants to the floor.

"Oh, my Mr. President, whatever shall I do with

that?" Gladys feigned shock at Mike's nudity. Gladys dropped to her knees before her husband's erect cock. She pulled her dentures out with one hand, and grabbed her husband's wrinkled, yet firm, phallus with the other.

"Gum job, baby. You know what your President likes!"

They didn't notice the rancid stench of death, creeping into their room.

Yet.

.

Anyone walking down the hall could hear Gladys and Mike fucking when they passed the elderly couple's apartment. Sean and Meghan were far too familiar with the sounds and recognized them immediately. Meghan wrinkled her nose, and Sean shook his head.

"Happy birthday, Mr. President," Gladys's muffled words seeped out from behind the door.

"God bless them," Sean said, "pew. Smell that?" Meghan grimaced in response.

"Yeah, they need to get the sewer lines fixed or something." He pushed open the door to their mother's apartment. The muffled sounds of Mike moaning in pleasure seeped through the wooden door.

"If you say so," Meghan replied.

"If you say so what?" Maureen asked from her sitting chair.

"Oh nothing, Mom." Meghan said, "It's your neighbors. They're being loud again."

"I know, I can hear them," Maureen didn't look pleased with this.

"Anyone walking down the hall can," Sean said. The three of them got a chuckle out of this," and moved to the kitchen table. Sean helped his mother along, and she took his arm without fussing.

"Thank you," she said.

"I love you, Mom, I'll do anything for you."

"I know you will."

"That's why we told the Para-Hunters you don't want to talk to them."

"Para-Hunters? Why would they want to talk to me?"

"Because they heard you saw Dad's ghost the other day and they somehow think it's related to the strange deaths on the property," Meghan said.

"What ghost? What deaths? What are you talking about?" A sheen of confusion covered Maureen's face. Her children saw this on multiple occasions. They knew it indicated a genuine memory loss.

Sean recounted the events of the last couple of days, up to their meeting with the production team. The death of her doctor, the bizarre circumstances around Marion Webster and Richard James. None of it brought any reaction from Maureen.

"What's for dinner?" Sean changed the subject. He watched his mother shrug.

"I didn't take anything out of the freezer today."

"Why don't we order out?" Meghan suggested.

"That would be nice," Maureen agreed. Meghan pulled her cell phone out and tapped at it.

"Mom, what was the name of the Italian seafood place you mentioned to me? Was it Bella's? I can't find it on google," Meghan said and looked up from her phone.

"What are you talking about?" Maureen said.

"No. No. The other day, the calamari we had, Mom, you said you got it from Bella's. Wasn't that the name?"

"No, I didn't. I've never heard of a place called Bella's. We ate calamari? I don't remember that, either. Are you kids playing tricks on this old lady now? Was it good?"

This exchange made the reality of their mother's state evident. Neither sibling wished to answer her. Both feared breaking down in tears if they spoke. After a few moments, Meghan spoke up.

"You don't mind if we stay the night, do you, Mom?" Sean shot Meghan a stern, unapproving glance, then his body language recanted when he realized where she was leading.

"Why of course, I'd love it if you did, it's better when you're closer," Maureen replied.

"We don't trust those Ghost Hunter people to not come knocking if they see us leave," Sean added. Meghan nodded in agreement.

"Then it's a sleepover!" Meghan declared, and the three of them belly laughed together.

It would be the last joy they'd experience as a family.

•

Gladys made sure she locked the door today. SummerHome was becoming a dangerous place to live. First the Doctor, then Mr. Maddox, and now the janitor and Mrs. Webster. RJ would always be kind and helpful to Gladys and Mike. She heard stories about him after he and Mrs. Webster were discovered in Apartment One. The whispers spoke of the inappropriate positions their dead bodies were discovered in. Gladys shivered at the thought. After all, Marion was only a few years older than her and Mike.

She chose not to believe the rumors.

She put on her best blonde wig and white dress and went to play with her husband.

Gladys preferred to take Mike bent over, doggy style. She never cared for being smothered under his large frame. When he fucked her from behind he filled her and stimulated all the nerves. She found at her ripe old age, they still made her quiver.

Her bladder dropped sometime in her late forties and she'd worn incontinence pads for decades. The bedroom ramifications of this meant she squirted with every thrust. Mike didn't mind her pissing all over him, it came out sterile. She knew it turned him on more.

"Fuck me, Mr. President, fuck me!" Gladys screamed. Mike obliged his wife's demands and thrust into her as deep as he could.

"Here comes my Cuban missile, baby!" Mike shouted in response.

"Yes! Come in my oval office, Mr. President!"

•

Down the hall, in apartment seven, Cindy Huther rinsed the bits of food sticking to her dentures off in the sink before placing the prosthetic in their overnight wash. This nightly ritual went off like normal, except Cindy wouldn't leave her bathroom.

When she turned around she noticed a puddle on the floor. It caught her by surprise, she must have wet herself. Then she saw the pinkish swirls in the urine.

"That can't be good," she said, knowing she'd have to call the nurse's aide. She tried stepping over the pool. It wasn't the best decision she'd made in her life. Cindy lost her balance and fell, striking her head on the sink before smashing her face into the ceramic tiling on the bathroom floor. The bones in Cindy's face shattered on impact. She was knocked out cold, which was good. Cindy slowly exsanguinated from the wound, dying in place before she could be burned.

•

Mike did as commanded, arching his back and holding his thrust. The palpitations from the orgasm caused his entire being to shake and for a moment he feared he might die. Gladys pushed back into him and moaned in response. He relaxed, no longer on the cusp of death, closed his eyes, and enjoyed the rush.

As he spasmed, Mike could feel Gladys gripping his cock with the walls of her vagina, milking him dry. He never tired of his wife's bedroom skills, not once in the sixty years they'd been together. He pulled out. The room air temperature, not quite as warm as the interior of Gladys's vagina, cooled and tickled his still throbbing organ.

He waited for Gladys to finish him off. She loved to lick his shaft clean after fucking, before sucking out all the remaining jizz in his urethra like it was a toothpaste tube, as he softened in her mouth. Mike opened his eyes, looked down, and didn't see what he expected to.

Was he losing it?

Gladys somehow disappeared. Instead of his wife, a woman he didn't immediately recognize knelt before him.

Wait! I know her! He thought back, *yes!* He did remember her.

Moira Cunningham?

Did he die? He must have because Moira died long ago, he knew this, in Syracuse. She died so young, in her sixties. He went behind Gladys's back to attend the funeral. If she knew he'd given a shit about a rival dying, it might muck up their whole relationship. What was it, thirty years ago?

Moira, he recalled their summer fling while Gladys was away, and nothing more. The slightly older married woman, much more experienced than he. She encouraged him to marry Gladys, which he did. He never told her because, well, he doubted Gladys would ever understand. He lived with the skeleton in his closet.

But now it was kneeling before him sucking on his dick, and she looked the same as she did in college. She popped his cock out of her mouth.

"You know what I did to the baby you gave me?"

Baby? What baby, Mike wondered to himself until blurting out, "What are you talking about? What baby?"

"Our baby, the one I never told you about. Why else would I have fucked you like I did? We needed it and when we were done with it, we let it burn in a fire!"

"What? Who are you talking about?" Mike's heart raced and pounded in his chest.

•

An angel of death continued to reap throughout SummerHome, providing the sacrifices required to feed the fae magic at use. Muriel Brownell fared no better in apartment twelve. The nightmares came as they always did, with or without the assistance of ghostly gray tabbies.

And though Muriel's brain had grown accustomed to the rigors of fending off the memories of her ex-husband, her heart could no longer take the stress. The last thing her body allowed Muriel was a reprieve from the vision of his leering visage, salivating at tying her and beating her. Instead, she is greeted by the smiling face of her dead daughter, forgiving Muriel for her weaknesses.

Muriel Brownell expired in her sleep, not knowing the part she played in a centuries-old ritual.

G ladys happily gobbled on her husband's throbbing cock, giving the gum job to end all gum jobs. She closed her eyes and tickled the bottom of the shaft with her tongue, the way he liked it. She knew he liked it because it made him twitch. But this is the first time she'd watched his eyes roll into his head-

And turn black.

"Mike? Are you Okay? Mike?" She asked, trying not to alarm him. Her husband stood still, unmoving. Fear for her husband gripped Gladys in an invisible vice. Her first instincts told her this was some reaction to the ED pill.

She hoped.

She was wrong. Oh, so horribly wrong.

Mike fell forward, crashing into the coffee table. The table collapsed as his face smashed into the wood and glass. Gladys found herself trapped underneath her husband. His cock thrust deep down her throat. He convulsed in the death throes of his heart-attack and came, pumping more come than she had ever known him to. Frail, she was unable to push her dead husband off her. Mike O'Connor choked his Mrs. with his medically engorged cock. The makers of the pharmaceutical may have been proud to learn their medicine worked after death. The fluids went down the wrong pipe, drowning Gladys in semen and urine as his bladder released, and she joined her husband in the afterlife.

The ritual's sacrifices spilled the blood needed for the transference to be complete.

CHAPTER 19: Never Trust a Witch

"**A**re you sure you want to spend the night?" Maureen asked her children as they tucked her into bed.

"Yes, Mom," Sean and Meghan answered in unison, "Love you."

"Love you, too," Maureen replied. The siblings turned the light off and closed her door as they exited into the living room.

"You can take the guest room, Meg," Sean said.

"Are you sure, you had a rough day," his sister replied.

"I'm going to take a shower and wrap myself up in a blanket on the couch, plus if someone knocks on the door, I'll be closest to the door. Since I sleep in the buff, if it happens to be the nosey Ghost Hunters, they'll get something to show on TV.”

“Hah! If their camera can focus on things that small,” Meghan quipped. Sean shook his head and smiled.

“Thank you, sis. For everything tonight. Really. The night is turning out better than the day,” he then excused himself to take a long-needed, therapeutic shower.

“Good night, don’t let the ghost hunters bite,” Meghan added as she walked off to the guest bedroom. She stopped at the kitchen on the way, poured a glass of water straight from the tap, and drank it down. Sean noted she didn’t fill the glass and empty it first.

“Finally broke that habit?” He asked.

“Huh?” Meghan shook her head not understanding her brother’s question.

“Never mind, it’s nothing,” Sean shrugged his shoulders, and Meghan, her thirst quenched, turned in for a restful sleep.

This wouldn’t be the case.

•

Sean sat on the toilet, processing the past few day’s events as he ran the shower on hot, fogging up the bathroom mirrors and glass surfaces. The end result was his personal steam bath and an immediate destressing from the day's events.

The relief of talking to his sister set him at ease. He could finally relax after a shit day. Still, one thing nagged him since the incident with the trucker more than the Para-hunters.

What did it mean? Sean thought *Blood is reaped and sewn?* The phrase echoed in his head. He closed his eyes and the memory of the bloody mess surrounding the trucker returned to haunt him. He could see the bright orange-red, covering the tiles of the bathroom floor. Sean closed his eyes, hoping it would black out the imagery.

It didn't.

The imagery came to life in vivid detail.

"Jesus Christ," he spoke aloud and sighed; stood from the toilet, pulled the curtain back, and stepped into the hot shower. The water massaged him and Sean gasped in pleasure. The din of the spray cascading off his back drowned away the mental horror show attempting to invade his psyche. Soon it was gone, replaced with positive thoughts.

Blood is reaped.

Yeah? But I saved a man's life! Sean reminded himself as he turned the water off, patted himself dry with a towel, and followed his sister's lead in going to bed. He did as he promised earlier, and wrapped up in a blanket, nude on the couch. Within minutes of laying down, he fell asleep. The nightmares waited to start later; but not in his dreams. Sean's subconscious kept his dreams a secret unto itself. Outside, in the halls of SummerHome, they flourished.

Blood is sewn!

•

Meghan slept in the guest room, and dreamed, too. Like her brother, she fell asleep the moment her head touched the pillow. The dreaming started soon after. The memories of the day were processed first, before dissolving into frantic visions of terror.

Her nightmares on this night were not her own. They were far older than she could fathom, and doused in the rains of sacrifice.

•

Salt rides on the air and an empty courtyard beckons Meghan. A cotton gown covers her otherwise naked body. She carries a sickle in one hand and grasps the arm of a man with the other. Her bare feet feel the morning dew in the grass. She recognizes this place, but cannot place it at first. Tall poles, a baker's dozen in total, line the interior in a circle. Tall grass grows up the sides of the poles.

At the base of seven of the poles is a pile of human bones, picked dry of meat and bleached white by the sea salt and sun. The skulls of the deceased are encircled with wreaths of now dried flowers. This jogs Meghan's memory, she knows where she stands.

Isle Magee's monastery courtyard.

A cramp fills her insides with pain. She bends over in agony and realizes this is no normal cramp. Her belly is extended and full.

I'm pregnant? Meghan's dream reveals.

"Is everything well, my love?" John Magee asks.

"Aye," Meghan replies. But it's not Meghan's voice. It's Mary Brigit Dunbar's, "the children will come in spring."

"Twins, as foretold."

"Aye, as foretold. One for me and one for the fae."

"We are booked on the first passage to the new world tomorrow as Husband and wife, John and Biddy Magee. I have secured us a tract of land from a Dutchman, in the province of New York, near the shores of an inland lake. We'll be far from the eyes of those who may hunt us," John slapped the satchel he carried with their legal papers.

The lovers embrace. Meghan feels John Magee hold her in his arms. It's comforting and soothing until Mary

Brigit allows Meghan in on her plan. She has no other option but to do so. Meghan is all too aware of the sickle grasped in her hand.

John Magee stumbles away from his lover, his eyes wide open, staring at his murderer.

His new wife.

"I'm sorry my love. I never told ye, but it was always meant to be this way," Mary Brigit says with Meghan's tongue, "the spell asked for a 13th sacrifice, the father of the firstborns. Now it's complete. For now. I'm so, so sorry."

John Magee can't speak. He mouths words, cursing the woman who betrayed him. Blood runs down his neck and blends with his black overcoat and tunic.

NEVER TRUST A WITCH, his lips form the words, and Meghan feels them stabbing her like John Magee's black rapier.

"You'll soon do the same thing to the father of your firstborns," Mary Brigit, no- she's Biddy Magee now and forever more-says to Meghan, "the blood is reaped, my dear. And the blood is... sewn."

CHAPTER 20: College Days

JD Thompson sat in the production van with his daughter going over the video footage from the day's interviews. Hours upon hours of talking to crazy old people, not a single one of them ever seeing a real ghost or having a supernatural experience they could expand upon. His irritation with how things had gone was showing. Sam picked up on this.

This," he gestured at the video monitors, "this is all shit. I have fucking jack shit to use as the centerpiece of a fucking episode. A jacket. Ted won't let us use the footage of Elaine freaking out. We needed to get that interview with the Coleman woman," he said and punched the desk. The entire rig of electronics attached to it shook and flickered.

"Please don't break the editing machine, it's the only one we've got and we can't get them overnighted from Amazon," Sam told her father.

"You're a little too smug for your own good sometimes," JD said. He couldn't stand his daughter, she was a goddamn liberal and it annoyed him to no end. But she was a good producer and one of the few who would work with JD. His ultra-right wing, conspiracy theory-laden politics got him in trouble on more than one occasion. He didn't care.

"And your mouth has ruined more interview opportunities and convention appearances than I care to talk about, today's being a classic for the record books. At least you didn't bring up reptilians. This time."

"Very funny."

"Hey, you're the one who has Alex Jones on speed dial in his contacts, not me."

"Even fucking funnier, and remind me why I work with you, once again?"

"I'm your daughter, and I'm the only producer who will work with you. Not to change the subject, but the other resident who passed recently, Mr. Maddox, his apartment is vacant and set up as a showroom. The director gave us permission to stay in the vacant apartment the next couple of nights while we're shooting the episode."

"What about Ted and Elaine? I doubt she'll want to stay in the building overnight."

"They can stay in their hotel rooms, they're paying for them, Elaine insisted they stay at the Super-8, of all places, she refuses to stay here like you said. We don't have to listen to Ted bitch about his ass itching. You can get set up in the apartment, and I'll go over there for the voiceovers I want to get done tonight."

"Okay by me, not like it's the first murder house we've ever spent the night in," JD said, "sure it won't be as nice as the mansion in the Catskills we stayed at last year, but anything to come in under budget I'll take."

"You know the Balloon Boy killer is incarcerated at the mental hospital in this town, right?" Sam raised an eyebrow as she spoke and pointed to a mystery location outside of the van.

"Holy shit, that's right, we are in Fenton, aren't we? I'm sorry, we go to so many locations they all blur together. Wait. Didn't you go to state college here?" Sam nodded, pursing her lips, evidently impressed her dear old Dad remembered another connection to the town, "Well, that's good, you can catch up with old friends and I think I'll pass on giving that nut job a second visit. The video footage of him creeped me out enough for a lifetime. I can't watch game shows because of him."

"Tell me about it. Alrighty then, Dad. I'll see you later.

I have that voice-over work to do with Elaine. Tomorrow's the big day here, so I won't be too-too late," Sam replied as she exited the production van.

"Big day, indeed!" JD grumbled a goodbye, faking enthusiasm, and gave her a confirming thumbs-up behind her back. He rolled his eyes. He didn't expect her to come back. She never did. He knew where she was going.

He should have said goodbye. It would be the last time JD Thompson would see his daughter.

•

A twenty-minute drive in bad traffic and catching lights would take Samantha to the Super 8. She was starving and knew a few places in Fenton she could get a good meal. Sam had plenty of time, and the joy of being a behind the camera producer was, no one knew who the fuck you were. Sam could eat in public under the aegis of anonymity.

The producer shook her head, trying to get the visions of the cat out of it. She still didn't know what she saw in the apartment. In all the time they had done this show together, she'd never seen anything as unnerving. Samantha Thompson didn't scare easily. But...

The Goddamned cat.

She'd seen apparitions before, but none so crisp and clear, and only through the camera's monitor. It stared back at her. Something loomed in its eyes, something scrambled and discordant. It terrified Sam when she finally focused on it.

Her reflection.

Sam really couldn't stand Fenton. It was a dirty shithole of a city to her and she hated most every day she spent in college here at SUNY FCC, or Fenton Correctional Compound, as the students lovingly bequeathed their alma Mata. Long the butt of inbreeding jokes, most of them racially charged and pointed at the local Onondaga population, the small city on Lake Ontario was as far out of the way as it could be, isolating its residents.

She remembered going up there for a "comic book convention" at the college, returning a favor from a classmate. It turned into a veritable waste of time and gas. Boasting a group of last-minute no-shows, has-been talent, not to mention an exuberant entrance fee for a handful of vendors selling re-gifted, over-priced merchandise, Swamp City Con had been aptly named. Or Swamp Shitty Con, as she called it.

Perhaps the anger had lingered in her due to the association she had with a promoter of the event. One of her friends, a local comic book shop owner, and social activist, had invested heavily in the convention and thought five hundred people walking through the turnstile on a Saturday was a good turnout. She mentally commended him on his optimism, noting he would probably be the person she would also go to for unsolicited positive comments the next time she found her self-esteem buried in a blanket of depression.

The cat stared at her with those eyes. They knew her deepest, darkest secrets. And it went as far as to strike Elaine.

It knew everything about them.

Sam started shaking, it always happened this way, her memories triggering an anxiety attack. She felt her palms sweating and the room became a kaleidoscope of sounds and colors. She focused on the road and wasn't ready to have an emotional breakdown.

Yet.

CHAPTER 21: Sacrifices

The sacrifices continued throughout SummerHome. In the Drakes' apartment, a sleepwalking Bill acted out his dreams, again. This time, unlike the nights before, his actions were far more visceral.

Babs was splayed out on the bed in the Drake's bedroom. Bill sat on top of her, straddled across her chest massaging her face with his hands. Pink, black and red ichor covered his arms up to the elbows. Bits and pieces of a shattered cement brick encircled Babs' head.

Or at least what used to be her head.

Smoke filled the apartment and leaked into the bedroom. The headboard of their bed was home to a crude fingerpainting declaring BILLY LOVES BABS inside a fingerpainted heart. Instead of oils and paints; bits of brains and coagulating blood made up the color palette of Bill Drake's work of art.

He marveled at it for a moment, as the smoke filled the room, before standing on the bed in an attempt to dismount his wife's corpse. Bill coughed, found he couldn't breathe, and slid to the side. He banged his head off the headboard, adding one last touch to his masterpiece. He marveled at it from the floor before succumbing to a combination of smoke inhalation and blood loss from his cracked open skull.

•

Down at the end of the hall in apartment twenty, VIP Dave and Caryn *(aka Carry)* Brooks slept. The couple went to bed early, not realizing they, too, would be both a tool and a part of the sacrifices required on this night.

Before hitting the sack, Dave walked their dogs, as he did every night. Tonight, the dogs were exceptionally antsy, and Dave couldn't wait to stick them in their makeshift kennel. He didn't see the gray tabby cat sneak into their apartment with them after Dave walked the dogs and cleaned off Sammy's asshole. The dogs saw the intruder, and reacted in kind, whining and growling so much Dave and Carry put headphones on to drown them out.

Before going to bed, Dave penned them up as usual in the kitchen. The gates didn't stop the gray tabby cat from jumping up onto the kitchen counter and taunting the dogs further. This drove the dogs into a yipping frenzy, but Dave and Carry couldn't hear it in their bedroom with headphones streaming ambient rainstorm noises.

Sammy could stand on his hind legs midway up the second baby gate, and reach the countertop.

Or the stove.

The ghostly cat jumped from the counter to the stovetop. Sammy swatted at it, missed, and turned the burner on, except the pilot didn't catch. Natural gas flooded the apartment for the next hour while the cat continued to play games with the dogs. The gas intoxicated Dave and Carry in their sleep, sending them into a deeper, dreamless slumber they'd never wake from.

The cat continued to taunt the dogs. Sammy jumped at it and hit another burner with his paw. It clicked until the pilot lit.

This time, the burner came to life.

There was a brief moment where the blue flame of

the gas stove flickered, and the conscious dogs stared at it. They didn't understand they should be terrified. Fortunately for them, it didn't last long. The dogs, along with anything flammable, were incinerated. An audible whoosh resonated through the apartment as the fire sucked up the remaining oxygen. The apartment turned into an inferno, VIP Dave and Caryn joined their pets a few seconds later.

And the cat, you ask?

Intangible and impervious to flames, the ghostly feline licked a paw and cleaned its head, before phasing through the door.

The fires followed a spread throughout SummerHome unabated.

CHAPTER 22: Sex and Magic

Quiet and serene halls greeted JD Thompson within SummerHome, giving him a new perspective on the facility. Once inside, he discovered he wouldn't need much. JD walked into the Maddox apartment to assess what he might need to bring in from the van for amenities.

He read the old man lived in Apartment six for twenty years, ever since the facility opened. But these two decade-long relationships meant little to the corporate masters of SummerHome. They didn't waste any time in clearing his stuff out. JD was lucky to pay off an orderly for the jacket and scarf.

The place was pristine and pre-furnished with donations from the Donahue furniture store's college Leasing Department. JD settled in quickly. He tossed his toiletry bag into the bathroom, picked a bedroom, and got ready for bed. A long, steaming shower later, he dried off, cracked his bedroom door a hair, like he always did, and went to bed. The light of the bathroom sent a sliver of luminescence into the bedroom. JD may have been a ghost hunter, but it never changed one thing about him.

He was afraid of the fucking dark.

His mother, Dot Johnson, God bless her abusive soul, thought it appropriate to scare her young son into coming in at sundown, alongside her other less than nurturing parenting techniques. She raised him like he was a business venture and not a child. The Johnsons lived next door to a cemetery, and little JD often played in the graveyard.

"The ghosts will get you!" His mother would tell the pre-teen JD. This evolved into a serious fear of the dark, and the reason he became a ghost hunter in the first place, to show himself nothing was there.

Ghosts are bullshit, people are the real monsters. JD's mother created a schism. He'd spent years-decades-on his paranormal quest, only to realize the true monster was Dot Johnson.

His head hit the pillow, and JD Johnson fell asleep, safe and secure under the watchful eye of the bathroom's light.

He never saw the gray tabby cat, hiding in the

shadows on the other side of the light line. Its presence drew the nightmares JD would soon be living. While the man slept, the cat sat, flicking its tail patiently.

Watching.

Waiting.

For the line to disappear.

•

Sam parked her car in front of Elaine's room at the Super-8. She didn't bother bringing any of the day's work with her when she exited the vehicle. Instead, she took her time and slowly walked up to Room 109.

They're always ground floor for her. Sam noted when she stood before the door. She knocked but opened the door without waiting for a response. A set of candles were lit on the desk, giving off the only light in the room. Elaine sat on the edge of her bed in her frumpy, Nana nightclothes.

"It's about time. It's getting to be way past my bedtime. I normally turn into a pumpkin at 11:00," Elaine chastised Sam.

"I'll give you a pumpkin pie instead, how's that?" Sam replied as she closed the door behind her. Elaine chuckled.

"I bet you will," Elaine said, "JD is busy working?"

"As always. He thinks we're working on voiceovers."

"Oh, there's going to be some voiceovers tonight, that's for sure," Elaine winked at Sam.

"I got him set up in one of the apartments at SummerHome."

"I don't like the feel of that place, I'm sorry," Elaine said, shaking her head, "Oh, hell no, I don't like it. And after what I saw-"

"We saw, don't forget that," Sam added.

"Okay, we saw, I think we've earned some stress relief."

"Yes, we have. Where's Ted?"

"In bed, sleeping on the third floor. He took his meds and they knocked him out cold like they always do. They couldn't give us rooms next to each other."

"Is that so? That's a shame."

"It is," Elaine spread her legs further apart and hiked her nightshirt up. Samantha moved in front of her and dropped to her knees, "you know what that means?" Samantha nodded and smiled.

"The voiceovers can be as loud as we want?" Sam asked, already knowing the answer.

"You bet your ass they can be!" Elaine declared and put her hands on Samantha's head. Sam, in turn, placed her hands on each of Elaine's thighs and slid them along the woman's legs. Elaine's nightshirt rode with Sam's fingers, up to her pelvis, exposing her shaved pubic area and vulva. She glistened in the candlelight.

"Somebody's wet," Sam said, licking her lips. And like moments before when she arrived, she didn't wait for a response before going in.

·

Ted Buffett peeked out the curtain of his room on the second floor of the Super-8. He saw the car pull up in front of his wife's hotel room and wasn't surprised to see Samantha Thompson exit the vehicle a few minutes later. He wasn't stupid. He knew what would be going on in the room.

Ted fell in love with Elaine the day he first saw her in high school. When she confided in him about her visions of the dead, it spurred an interest in the paranormal in the teenager. The opportunist in him also saw a chance for them to get rich off of her secret talent.

Ted knew the only way he would be able to remain part of the equation was to immerse himself in the paranormal. He studied everything from Ancient aliens and mythology to theology, ESP, and telekinesis.

Eventually, he became an unofficial expert, a walking dictionary, in the field of paranormal investigation.

This interest remained with him. He became a regular guest on Coast-to-Coast AM in recent years as a result, often consulted for any topic in the paranormal. Though Ted wasn't sure if this was because of his experience or his exposure.

Ted and Elaine went to college together, with Elaine getting a liberal arts degree. Ted, however, studied business management while minoring in broadcast television, eventually getting a BA in both fields. They watched the Warrens rise to fame and emulated them, becoming as popular as their influences.

It started falling apart about ten years before now when the Buffetts started sleeping in separate bedrooms at home. Elaine claimed she couldn't handle Ted's snoring. This practice carried on to separate hotel rooms. The stipulation of neighboring or conjoined rooms would become less and less of a priority as the years went by.

A few years later, Ted and JD caught on to Elaine and Samantha's extracurricular activities. Neither man, to this date, had approached the women about it. Both of them agreed a confrontation would certainly spell doom for their production. As long as it didn't interfere with their work or the quality of the show, they'd keep the knowledge in their back pockets.

It was also why Ted took sleeping pills.

Ted Buffett still loved his wife dearly, and the stress of keeping this knowledge to himself took its toll on him. He played the doting husband despite wanting to just leave. But he knew Elaine and knew she was the real deal because she could actually see fucking ghosts. She, not him, was the breadwinner, something he always understood since the day she confided in him. He remembered what happened to John from 'John & Kate Make Eight,' after he fooled around and she found out.

He should be researching what happened earlier in the day at SummerHome. He'd never experienced something like this with her before.

And it scared him so much he was afraid to look.

Instead, he sat on the edge of the bed with a glass of water held in one hand, and the pills grasped in the palm of the other. The bullshit in the nursing home today pissed him off. There was no way in hell he was allowing them to use the footage of Elaine's seizure. He threw the pills back in his mouth and swallowed a huge gulp of water. He sighed, then yawned, and put the glass on the nightstand.

Ten minutes later he was fast asleep.

It wouldn't last.

CHAPTER 23: The Transference

After the kids tucked her in, Maureen fell asleep. For the first time in oh, so long, silence graced the inside of Maureen Coleman's head. No more constant chatter, creating an ambient stream of white noise in the back of her mind. For the first time in forty-five years, Maureen knew peace and her thoughts.

What she didn't expect was to be woken up by the appearance of a presence in her room. She clenched her eyes closed, afraid of who might be there, caring not to see any more apparitions the like of John Magee. Maureen's heart raced, she dared not imagine what horror entered the room. A few tense moments passed where her heart pounded in her frail chest so strongly she feared she may crack her ribs or sternum.

Maureen opened her eyes, no longer able to keep

them closed. Her heart didn't relax when she saw her daughter. Maureen's lip quivered. Tears welled and dripped down her cheeks as fear of the inevitable seeped into her being.

"There ye be, mum," Meghan said in a voice not quite her daughter's. A voice Maureen knew all too well, "dun be afeared, mum. We're here to see ye through this."

"My poor Meghan," Maureen said, "I'm so sorry you're going through this."

"Meghan is sleeping, mum, she's not ready to join us. Not yet."

"She won't be herself anymore. She was so independent, I thought maybe, with me coming here, she might not have to be part of this."

"Ye know it's not the way. Ye went through it too, mum, or do ye forget? 'Tis like giving birth, aye?"

Maureen nodded. Indeed, the Transference shared similarities with childbirth. Horrible pangs a mind will condition itself to forget, like the excruciating cramps of labor, except in this case your mind is no more than a computer program. The cells in your brain are ripped apart and defragmented, partitioned, and restarted. Then your body wakes with a new user, or, more accurately, the *old* user, running the show.

Biddy Magee.

Meghan's body sat on the edge of the bed and stroked

her mother's hair.

"There, there, mum. Ye can sleep now. Ye deserve the rest," Meghan's mouth said as she consoled Maureen. The words spoken? They belonged to Biddy Magee. Meghan's hand touched her, but Meghan didn't control it. Maureen's heart slowed, she no longer panicked. Instead, she felt at ease, accepting the fate she knew awaited her as the Transference completed. The Coleman matriarch knew she wouldn't die, she knew she'd join the host, now residing within her daughter's shell of a body.

Maureen Coleman's breathing slowed as she remembered a summer day, long ago, in the garden behind the family home. The insects, swarming all over, landing on her. The daisies, chrysanthemums, and black-eyed Susans, her favorite flowers, spread out and grew like weeds. The sight and smell of them made Maureen happy. She took a deep breath, as deep as she could, sighed, and aspirated.

CHAPTER 24: Wet Dreams

The squeal of the hinge of the door opening, followed by the clicking of a latch, stirred JD from the nightmares of his youth. A light sleeper as a result of his phobia, any sound could wake him up. The smell of smoke from his dream leaked into the real world. Or at least he assumed it was from his dream. And was this his daughter returning from the voiceovers?

He was wrong... and he knew he was wrong. She never came back from the voiceovers. He knew what went on between Elaine and Samantha. He turned a blind eye to it.

So, who was it?

JD closed his eyes tight, feigning sleep, praying it wasn't the ghosts from the cemetery.

I was in before dark, damnit! I didn't break the rules!

His frantic thoughts said to him. JD could hear her breathe, hear her disrobing. Hear her presence grow closer to his bed, her breathing heavy and seductive. It couldn't be Samantha, she wouldn't walk into his bedroom. He peeked through the lids of his eyes. All he saw were shadows.

And flesh.

This wasn't his daughter.

Who was it?

"Shhhh," she said, breaking the silence, "I know you want me. I could see it in your eyes."

Who was she? How did I know her? JD thought, frozen with terror.

She pulled the bedroom door closed, blanketing the room in blackened shadows from the window. JD didn't recognize her voice. Obscured by the darkness, he couldn't make out her face but could tell the woman's head of hair was pulled up out of her face with a hair clip of some sort.

Silently, she climbed into bed with JD. Half paralyzed in fear and half aroused, he didn't do anything to stop her. He lay in the bed and trembled. He didn't know if it was from fear or excitement.

Or both.

Naked breasts swelled against his arm as the intruder's body shifted. She slid on top and embraced him. Soft hands caressed JD's hips. She spread her legs, sliding one to either side until she was straddling him. He felt her grind against his groin, bringing his cock to life. He noticed she was sliding back onto him. The moist, humid heat of her sex taunted his stiffening member, and it grew harder in anticipation.

"Feck me, Daddy," the woman said with a thick rolling Irish accent and sat back on his cock. He didn't recognize her voice, but it didn't matter. Everything about her turned him on. He couldn't repel her, so he did as she asked and fucked her. His first thrust met some resistance, but she pushed back, he felt the tip of his cock rip through her hymen.

A virgin? She's a virgin?

She replied with a squeal of pleasure as he entered her. She rode him in the darkness, bucking and moaning in ecstasy. JD thrust his cock deeper and deeper into his mystery lover. She gripped him in a lubricated vice of flesh with the walls of her vagina, moaning and cooing as her hips slapped against his thighs.

He rolled her over, keeping inside her as he did, and held her arms down. Her hair covered her face, continuing to hide her identity from JD. He arched his back and pushed in until he felt her erect clitoris poking at him.

"Come for me, Daddy, please come for me," she

begged him. The walls of her vagina contracted around the girth of his cock, telling him she was in the throes of an orgasm. They rolled over, again, and she sat back, milking him, her vaginal muscles twitching. He obliged her request and released, coming with her.

"Yes, yes, yes! Come for me Daddy!" She screamed as his cock pulsed and he released and squirted inside of her. She held his arms down, still bucking as she came, her ass cheeks slapping off JD's thighs in applause of their performance. His orgasm sent bolts of electricity up his spine.

She sat up and raised her hands behind her head, squirming in ecstasy as she rode him. His cock remained hard, almost as if they were locked together. He saw her hair fall over her face. The tips of its length tickled the tip of his nose.

"Blood is reaped," she said and fell on top of him. Before JD could process what she said, he felt a warmth across his chest.

He tried to speak, but couldn't. He threw his hands to his neck. Something wet splashed against his hands. The woman continued fucking him. His cock throbbed and he knew another orgasm was coming.

JD arched his back as he tried to breathe and found he couldn't. A garbled bubbling sound came from his throat. He tasted blood as it seeped into his mouth, choking him. He wanted to cough but couldn't. The blood poured out of his neck and down his throat, into his lungs. He felt his cock spasm and he came again, the pleasure and pain mixing and sending him into a euphoria he'd never felt before. He finally understood why the French called an orgasm La Petite Morte.

The Little Death.

"And blood is sewn." JD Thompson heard his murderer say before he closed his eyes he saw them, the ghosts from the cemetery. His mother was right, all those years ago.

They were waiting for him. All of them.

•

*E*laine...
Where are you, Elaine?
Help me! I'm lost, Elaine!

Elaine thoroughly enjoyed Samantha's skills at cunnilingus, it took her mind off the day's bullshit. All was fine until she heard a familiar voice call her from the otherside.

But whose voice? She wondered.

Elaine...

Already in a trance from her lover's skills at oral pleasure, the woman dropped into her *personal darkness* to hear the message more closely.

Elaine! She hears the words clear, albeit distant. She recognizes their source in the sub-realm of her personal darkness.

It's JD Thompson. *And this means he is dead. His neck is sliced open, and the flaps of skin move in conjunction with his lips as he speaks.*

"Blood is reaped and sewn!" JD's ghost says to her, repeating the phrase Elaine heard from the demonic cat in SummerHome. It sends a shiver up her spine. She watches her friend fade away into the light before her consciousness returns to the hotel room.

•

Elaine pushed Samantha's head out from between her legs.

"What the fuck?" Sam said, "what was that about?"

"Your father's dead."

"What?" Samantha looked stunned, "My father is dead? What the fuck? How do-"

"I didn't stutter, girl, the entity in that shithole did it," Elaine raised her voice over Samantha's, cutting her off, "we have to get Ted and go to SummerHome, now, or more people will die. Shit, I think we're too late already, but we have to try."

"What do you mean?"

"I finally got the skinny and figured this bullshit out. This is dark fae at work. The old gods, Sam, they never died. They went under the mound," Elaine said as she got dressed, "and once one of them comes out, it'll do anything it can to stay in our world."

"What do you mean?"

"I do believe someone—something—inside SummerHome is a fairie changeling!"

Part Three

Witchwood & Iron

CHAPTER 25: Old Gods Never Die

Trapped within her own mind, Meghan couldn't move, but she could see much more than anticipated. Everything secret hidden by the witch, an open book for her to read, with all she needed to know about Biddy Magee and her host. Right back to the beginning, three centuries ago.

After all, the fondest memories are saved first.

These Mounds could be found throughout the Emerald Isle. They said the Tuatha de Danann fled under the Mound and became the little people when the Christians came. A mound near the village, long rumored to be a fairy den, often attracted local youths seeking adventure.

Like the other mothers in the village, Mary Brigit

Dunbar's mother warned her to stay away from the hill and the cave for years. She told the familiar fable of how the cave has a bottomless pit within, leading straight to Hell. True or false, the tale worked.

As she grew into a woman, Mary Brigit, often accused by others of being too smart for her own good, found this story to be preposterous.

Until she heard the song, breaking the still of the midsummer night. 'Twas a haunting melody, dynamic and beautiful. It resonated over the fields and across the hills, permeating the air and ground. It seeped through the windows and walls of the County's dwellings, soothing some who heard it. Terrifying others. The latter knew from whence it came, and wished to never hear its mournful wail again.

In her family's cottage, the song invaded Mary Brigit's dreams during her first sleep. It swam about within her subconscious, transforming from sound into a swirling, gaseous form.

A cat, a big gray tabby. Its chest was adorned with a white diamond. It walked out of her dreams.

And she followed.

The young woman obtained a candle, ventured out, chasing the ghostly cat after her mother fell asleep, and went inside the mound anyway.

What Mary found in the cave was far from

leprechauns or sprites of lore. The floor was littered with animal bones, bits of cloth, pottery, and weathered parchment. The walls, painted in vast murals, depicted a paradise in the clouds populated with dark-skinned people all dressed in elegant clothes. She marveled at the beauty of the art until the flame of the candle exposed more than paintings.

Mary felt her heart jump when the eyes of an animal reflected in the light. A large feral cat, gray with a white diamond on its chest emerged from the shadows. It stood before a recess in the back of the cave, which Mary could now see housed an altar of sorts. The cat leaped down and rubbed against Mary's leg, mewing verse in the teenager's mind.

"My name is my own secret. But ye can call me Sabhdh," the cat said to her, before presenting a riddle to the girl who was not quite a woman yet.

"Free me and the bounty be,

"The secret to thrice times thrice

"Lives for thee."

Then the spectral cat walked away and disappeared into the darkness. The words repeated in her head over and over until Mary set the candle sconce on the altar. The flame lit up the enclosure, revealing a large feline skull sitting near the center. The white teeth of the bone smiled back at Mary and the green quartz cat's eyes twinkled in the center of each of the skull's eye sockets. She removed the skull from the altar, cradled it in her arm, secured her candle, and left the cave.

Once outside, Mary was shocked to find a full-grown cat in her grasp. She gasped and released the animal. It fell to the earth on four feet as would any other cat. The beast mewed, and Mary Brigit could again understand the sounds. She would never-could never- forget them.

"Thrice times thrice lives for thee

"Give unto me

"Seven maidens blessing the dawns ye'll rise

"With a shower of rain and dew.

"Seven lords calling the moons ye'll see,

"Thy first born's sire, in the act of desire,

"For the tolls of the midnight bell.

"The final gift be the sweetest,

"The first born taken

"From thy womb shall be forsaken

"When blood is reaped and sewn."

And the spell was cast. Meghan wasn't surprised to learn Biddy knew all along what she was doing. A sacrifice for each life she lives- no. That's not the right word. For each life she possesses. Her mother's, her grandmothers' going back to Biddy's first female child. And now Biddy resided in Meghan's body.

Meghan wondered if Maureen was ever truly her

mother. If any of the real women who gave birth to her nurtured her and Sean. Or if their lives were run by Biddy Magee with the intent of grooming them for this time. In hindsight, now trapped within her psyche, Meghan believed it to be the latter.

She watched from the back recesses of her mind, as Biddy chased her brother through the halls of SummerHome. She could smell the smoke and knew a fire burned somewhere within the walls of the facility. She also knew who was responsible for the blaze.

Biddy liked to set fires to cover their tracks.

•

Taken from **"INFAMOUS WITCHES VOLUME II, THE 18TH CENTURY"** by Theodore Buffett © 1997. Currently out of print:

Legends and myths are rooted in all cultures. No matter their origin, often one can find similarities between disparate cultures. Cultures frequently with thirteen principal, polytheistic deities. The Tuatha de Nanan of Irish lore share similar adventures with the gods of Greek and Roman myths. This trail of commonality can be filtered down to individual gods and goddesses. Inanna in the Sumerian myths is often depicted as Diana by the Greeks.

Or, take, for example, the Teutonic goddess Angraboda, a combinate weather elemental, seducer, and devourer of wayward souls wandering the winter wastes. She shares traits with Ne-On-Yar-He of the Algonquin and Iroquois mythos, an entire continent away. Often depicted as a serpent or tentacled Kraken inhabiting river waters, she controls the winds, rains, and snow, seducing those foolish enough to venture out in inclement weather. These myths are separated by thousands of miles, including an ocean, yet we find this similarity.

·

If such an immortal deity did indeed exist, might it be ambivalent to the plight of its prey? Or would it defend its hunting grounds, as any predator might, divine or otherwise? Would it call the elements to batter the threat?

Across the Great Lakes, reaching into the furthest reaches of the north, the rain and wind answer a primordial call. The clouds roll across the vast flatlands of the northern tundra, coming to their mistress of cold and ice.

CHAPTER 26: Waking the Dead

Biddy rode on top of John Magee. She appeared innocent and pure, virginal with a halo of light encircling her head. The eternal sin of her bargain would need his flesh, as she saved herself for him and only him, desiring one thing. John's seed.

"Blood is reaped and sewn!"

Meghan Coleman watched Biddy slice open her husband's throat with a sickle on repeat from a front-row seat. The blood poured out of him until she opened her eyes and screamed in terror, hoping to end the vision. Her goal was ill met.

The nightmare didn't stop.

It got worse.

"NEVER TRUST A WITCH!" John Magee's final words resonated in her head.

Meghan opened her eyes and screamed out in

surprise. She didn't recognize where she was. She wasn't in the guest room at her mother's apartment. Instead, she was in a strange bedroom, nude, sitting on top of a blood-soaked dead man. Recognition brought on shock as JD Thompson's lifeless eyes stared back at her.

A warmth filled her body, a feeling of euphoria that was turning to disgust. She rubbed her crimson-stained hands across her belly. She could feel him dripping out of her. She knew she and JD fucked. The thought of it, of the man's dead body growing cold under her, repulsed her.

Oh, my fucking God! Did I sleepwalk and kill a man? How did this happen? I don't remember coming here! Meghan's thoughts sped up, the words colliding together, *OhmyGodOhmyGod!*

She gasped for air as she panicked and threw herself off the dead man, falling to the floor. Tears burst from her eyes as her anxiety peaked.

What should I do? She asked herself, *Come on! Come on, Meghan, what do you do?*

Ye could leave here before anyone comes knocking. Biddy Magee answered Meghan's thoughts.

"Get out of my head!" Meghan ordered the voice.

It's our head, now, my pretty little thing. Soon the sacrifices will be complete, the transference will be complete, and we will be reborn. The blood was reaped so it can be sewn.

Meghan tried to move, but she couldn't. A gray tabby cat emerged from the shadows and rubbed against Meghan's head. It licked the blood off her fingers and purred.

Meghan felt her hands move on their own, and pet the cat.

"Sabhdh, ye've been waiting for us, as ye always do, a loyal thing ye be," Biddy Magee said to her familiar with Meghan's mouth, petting the spectral feline with Meghan's hands.

No, not Meghan's.

They were Biddy Magee's, now.

Meghan, like her mother before her, could only watch.

"Oh, we're not going anywhere. we've been in here longer than ye knew, lass," Biddy said, and Meghan knew the witch wasn't lying.

•

A cramp in Sean Spencer's bowels woke him up from a deep slumber. He shook the cobwebs from his eyes. There was complete silence in the apartment, no ambient noise from the halls of SummerHome filtered through the walls. It was soothing. The clock on the microwave told him it was a quarter past midnight.

He saw the bathroom stood vacant, to his relief, and tiptoed past the closed door of his mother's bedroom, afraid he might wake her or his sister. He waited until he was inside the bathroom and the door was closed before he turned the light on.

The humidity from his earlier shower left a film of moisture on the bathroom's surfaces. This included the seat of the toilet. Cold and damp, he slid on the seat when he sat down and almost slipped off the toilet.

Just one more thing to add to the list of today's bullshit, he noted in his head as he settled down and got to business.

The worries of the day quickly returned, consuming his waking thoughts. Every weird thing leading up to the here and now flowed together. A demolition derby of thoughts mashing into one another, creating chaos in his head. He tried to think of other things, but nothing came to mind.

When he was done, Sean flushed and washed his hands. He turned the light off and closed the door behind him, hoping he didn't wake anyone. As he made his way back to the couch, he caught a whiff of something foul.

Is that me? He thought at first, then he noted the stench was strongest in front of his mother's bedroom. Did his mother shit herself in her sleep? He pushed the door open.

"Mom, everything-" he stopped himself mid-sentence when he saw his mother staring at the ceiling, unmoving. He flicked the light on. The glaze covering Maureen Coleman's eyes confirmed his suspicions.

"Oh no, Mom. No, not now, not already!" Tears grew in Sean's eyes. He went to her side and grabbed her hand. It was cold and stiff. Maureen Coleman, formerly Maureen Spencer, was dead.

"Mom? No! Mom!" Sean wept as he spoke, the words coming out in bubbles of snot.

Is this our fault? For bringing her here? Or is this what they meant by blood is reaped and sewn? Sean thought, *were those premonitions warning me of Mom's death?* He tried wrapping his head around this all the while he cried, and cried, and cried, grasping his mother's hand.

This was the first time Sean Spencer smelled death. The first time he'd seen it this close.

It wouldn't be the last time on this night.

•

A frantic pounding on the motel room's door, accompanied by someone screaming his name, invaded Ted Buffett's dreamless, drug-induced slumber. His head throbbed from the sleeping pills. Slow to move, and slower to gather his thoughts, he looked at the clock on the nightstand. The red LED lights declared it was just past midnight, 12:07 to be precise.

Who the fuck is waking me up two hours after I hit the sack? Ted wondered, then recognized the voices. It was Elaine and Samantha. *What's their problem?*

"Ted, open up! Ted! Wake up! Ted!" The women screamed in random unison as they pounded on the door.

"I'm awake, for fuck's sake, I'm awake! Let me put on some Goddamned pants," he said, unsure if he said it loud enough for them to hear over their racket. When they stopped knocking and screaming his name, he felt confident they heard him. His throbbing head felt grateful for some relief. He pulled on some jeans and a button-up shirt over his t-shirt and opened the door.

"Come on, finish getting dressed, and put some shoes on. We have to go to SummerHome," Elaine said.

"It's midnight, and I thought you didn't want to go back there," Ted said as he buttoned up his shirt.

"Something in that place killed my Dad tonight," Sam added. Ted froze in place, stunned at the revelation.

How could JD be dead? Did this place have killer fucking ghosts in it?

"She's right," Elaine added, "I saw his spirit."

"What, what do you mean something killed him?" Slack-jawed, he shook his head, not wanting to believe what he was hearing.

"Every person in SummerHome is in danger right now, we have to go there and warn them!" Elaine said with a slight tremor in her enunciation. Ted never heard her voice shake like this.

Elaine was genuinely scared of something.

"I'll start the car, you guys can ride with me," Sam said and left. Elaine closed the motel room door behind her as she walked inside.

"What's going on?" Ted asked, "what killed JD? Has anyone called the cops yet?"

"I don't even know if anyone knows he's dead outside of me. I'm pretty sure it's a changeling, an evil fairy, and it's killing people to remain in our world," Elaine told her husband. Ted listened to her as he finished getting dressed. "Somehow it's ended up at SummerHome, and I think it's trapped inside the property."

"How so?"

"I think it's The wrought iron fence surrounding the property. Fairies can't cross or even touch iron without it fucking them up."

"You're right, it would work," Ted agreed with his wife. He was proud of her for coming up with this on her own. "What does it look like? A person or an animal?"

"It has a person it's tethered, too, yes. But I think this one is a cat-sidhe, and it's what fucked me up earlier today."

"That's the cat Sam saw in the camera and swatted you?" He asked. Elaine nodded, "I had my suspicions then, but I was too worried about you."

"Do we know who it's tethered to?" Outside, the blaring of the horn of Samantha's Forester called them.

"I think so."

"Who?" Ted asked his wife.

"The Coleman woman," Elaine said, and they left.

·

Tears streaming down his cheeks, Sean threw open the guest room's door. To his surprise, he found the room, and most importantly the bed, to be empty. Meghan was nowhere to be found. This shocked him almost as much as the death of their mother.

Where is she? He wondered. This wasn't like Meghan to do this.

"Meg?" Sean called her name, yet no one answered. He looked in the closet, under the bed. His sister simply disappeared. He was sure he would have heard her leave the apartment. Or would he have?

Sean went back to his mother's bedroom, pulled a sheet over her face, and pressed the alarm calling a nurse's aide to the room. The red light pulsed. A few moments later, a knocking at the door broke the silence of the apartment.

"Hello? Mrs. Coleman, it's Dawn, the CNA, is everything okay? I'm coming in," the disembodied voice said from behind the door. Before Sean could answer her, the door opened. The night shift CNA, her hair pulled back in a ponytail, stood in the doorway. Sean was clad only in his boxers. The CNA turned her head away.

"I'm sorry, you're Mrs. Coleman's son, Sean, right? Is everything alright?"

"No, it's not, Dawn. My mother is dead," he answered, looking down at the floor and covering the fly in his boxers with his hands.

"No, she's not," another voice answered him-

Mom? It was his mother's voice. *But she was dead!*

A gurgling sound, like a kid sucking on a straw near the bottom of a milkshake at a burger joint, filled the room. His gaze still at the floor, he saw the CNA faceplant at his feet. A pool of blood spread out, flowing from her neck.

Sean looked up to see Meghan standing at the door, a small sickle in her hand. A drop of blood fell from its tip. She was naked but for a silk black robe, left open. Her torso and hands were covered in black, sticky blood.

"Meghan? Oh, my God, Meg, what are you doing? What did you do? You killed her! Holy fucking shit! Mom's dead and this? Oh, fucking no you didn't!"

"Calm down, lad, ye've so much to learn," it wasn't quite Meghan's voice. The words were round, and sing-song, almost Irish in their cadence. The different voice coming from his sister snapped him out of his hysteria.

"Why are you talking like that? You sound like," he hesitated before continuing, his voice shaking as he said the words, "like, well, Mom, you know when she attacked the doctor the other day."

"Aye, as we should sound. The doctor was of fae blood and we didn't need him sending us away to another facility, so Sabhdh marked him with our hand. The iron got him."

"Sabhdh? Marked him?"

"He had old blood, fae ancestors. Most of these technology wizards and doctors do."

"Meghan, this is crazy talk. Stop it. And put some clothes on."

"There is no more Meghan. Well, there will be as far as the public knows. But I'm not Meghan. I'm, *we*, are so much more. They're all in here, you know, the bits and pieces of the half-dozen grandmothers that came before your mother and your sister."

"What do you mean? Meghan, you- you're my sister. And Mom is fucking dead."

"No, we're not, son," Meghan's voice... *changed again*... Sean's mother's words came from her lips, "we're all in here," her voice changed, as if a radio dial had been turned, "It's alright, we still love ye." The words changed, morphing in pitch and key as they came out, ending with the same brogue accent as before.

"This is crazy! Wash up and put some clothes on, we have to call someone about Mom and, God, I can't believe you killed the nurse's aide! You're going to go to jail, that's fucking murder, my God, Meghan!" Sean covered his eyes with his arm and stepped back.

"She had it coming, they're all going to die here tonight, it was destined to happen now or later."

"What do you mean they're all going to die? Who the fuck are you?"

"Who we've always been. Some, like our first mum, called me Mary Brigit once, but we prefer the name we took when we became who we've always been. Biddy. It's what our first husband called us, short for me middle name, Brigit."

"We? What are you? Some ghost who possessed my sister? Is that why the ghost hunters are here?"

Meghan, rather, Biddy, laughed at this assumption

with a great smile on her face.

"Oh no, lad. We be no spirit, because of ye're sister, we be flesh and blood as ye can see."

"That's my sister's body."

"Not anymore. She's always been promised to us."

Sean stood with his back against the wall of the apartment. His sister, if he could call her his sister anymore, walked to him, exaggerating her stride and revealing more of her unclothed legs with each step. It became clear Meghan forgot to wear something under the black robe. Well, she wasn't Meghan anymore. To say she was now an extension of their mother, grandmother, whatever Biddy was, could be a more accurate assertion. Physically, her body was indeed Meghan's. But her mind? The bits making up the rest of her, it wasn't Meghan at all. It belonged to their mother, Maureen.

No, not Maureen, not their mother.

Biddy Magee and all her incarnations through the decades ran the show, it occurred to Sean.

They always did.

"This is just another cycle in the wheel, brother," she spoke with a bright, Irish brogue, rolling across her tongue, "did ye know twins run in the family?" Biddy asked, not seeking an answer, her intent made clear. The Witch of Isle Magee smiled and licked her red lips.

Sean Spencer turned his head, to find some means

of escape from the *No! This can't be happening!* Sean screamed in his mind and broke from the moment.

"No!" He screamed and pushed her away from him. She stepped aside, running her hands over her blood-soaked breasts, tracing her nipples with her fingertips. Meghan, or rather Biddy, licked her lips.

"Ye be the First Born, and we need ye to complete the ritual of transference. Playing hard to get I see," she reached back out to him with gore-covered arms.

"The First Born? What the fuck? Ya know what? Actually, I'm playing hard to get away from this bullshit!" Sean announced. He ducked under her arms, dodging her grasp, stepped over the dead CNA, and ran out of the apartment. The door slammed behind him, locking closed.

In the hallway, he could smell smoke.

A fire? But where? He wondered.

No smoke alarms were sounding off, he saw no fire or flames, and there was no haze or fog. Instead of seeking the source, he remembered the weirdness behind the door, and ran down the hall, heading to the exit.

•

She opened the door, and Biddy, Sabhdh at her side, followed Sean.

CHAPTER 27: Fire and Rain

The flames engulfed SummerHome's west wing. The residents of the four apartments in the section of the facility were the first sacrifices of the night. Starting with VIP Dave and Caryn. Babs and Bill and their neighbors fell to the flames, as well.

The blaze spread into the south wing, and with it went Helen Marcoux who ate chicken wings with a knife and fork because *"we have utensils for a reason,"* Island Tom, and, lastly, their neighbor 'Big' Connie Clarke, who was overweight and mostly bedridden with complications from diabetes. Every resident of SummerHome, each with their own story of being in the facility. All of them succumbed to Biddy's ritual fire, sacrifices to her dark-fae spell.

The smell of smoke filled the halls, followed by a

crackling. But no fire alarms sounded off, and no one ran about in a frenzy, screaming *"Fire!"* No one except for Sean Spencer and Biddy Magee, of course. They ran and walked through the hallways, the latter stalking the former. Biddy needed Sean, he didn't know why, he didn't care.

Any remaining residents were all sleeping sound or soundly dead, along with the overnight CNAs and the on-duty nurses. Biddy saw to their demise personally as she encountered them in the halls.

Her sickle was sharp and the sacrificial blood flowed from their screams.

Sean could hear random screeching end abruptly from somewhere in the expanses of SummerHome and knew another unfortunate soul had fallen to the witch's hand. Part of him wanted to warn the rest of the staff, but he knew it would be useless to try. The damn cat somehow saw to that. No, he needed to get out of here before he died inside it and get as far away from Biddy as possible.

A crack of thunder could be heard rolling outside in the distance. Underneath it, though, from inside SummerHome, he heard someone else shouting.

And it wasn't Biddy Magee.

"Hello! Is there anyone alive in here? We're here to help!" It was a man's voice, a voice he heard many times over the years on television. It was Ted Buffett's voice.

•

The Forester carrying Ted, Elaine, and Samantha arrived at SummerHome. They saw the back half of the apartment complex, engulfed in flames and dark clouds of smoke filling the night sky. There were no rescue vehicles in sight, or earshot. It was as if SummerHome existed in a bubble.

"This place is almost fully involved, why aren't there any fire engines here?" Sam said.

"It's the fae. It must have stopped the alarms," Ted said, "Crafty little bastard. Do you have cell service?" Sam looked at her phone. The 5G LTE logo glowed in the corner.

"I do. I'll dial 911."

"Good," Elaine said, "Sam, sit here and wait for us."

"We need the production van, it's parked over there," Samantha pointed to the van, "I'll get it started."

"Even better. Come on, Ted," the woman got out of the car, tugging her husband's sleeve.

"What are you doing?" He protested.

"We have to see if there's anyone to save."

"We're too old for this kind of hero bullshit, Elaine." Ted stepped out of the car and grabbed his wife by the shoulder. A cold wind blew in, giving them both a shiver. Giant rain droplets fell sporadically. A storm was coming, blotting out the stars and moon, and it looked to be a doozy. Thunder rolled on the horizon, over the lake, and they could see flashes of lightning in the distance. Sean saw a face in the clouds and wondered if this was old Marion's flying head coming to get them.

"Do I look like I fucking care how old we are, you middle-aged ninny?"

"Middle-aged ninny? Really, Elaine?" Ted said, stopping in place.

"Yes, my dear husband. People are in danger and we can help," Elaine scolded her husband, "come on, let's go! That fire's spreading and we're running out of time, plus it's starting to rain."

He relented and allowed her to lead him along. Defiant, Elaine dragged Ted into SummerHome, marching hand in hand, and without fear.

Inside the facility, the fires of hell ran amok. Smoke rolled across the ceilings, fogging out the overhead lights. Ted and Elaine covered their faces with their sleeves.

"Is anyone alive?" Ted shouted.

"Hello!" Elaine screamed, "Is anyone there? Hello!"

"Is anyone here?" Ted shouted louder, cupping his hands to his mouth.

"Hello?" Someone answered from down the hall, near the main intersection of the facility's wings, two of which were now fully engulfed in the blaze. They ran toward the voice. The person shouting came into view, running like a bat out of hell, away from the burning wings. Ted and Elaine instantly recognized him.

Maureen Coleman's son.

•

"Why did I know you'd show back up here?" Sean Spencer said when he ran into Ted and Elaine Buffett.

"It's what we do," Elaine said, "we investigate weird shit."

"This is some weird shit, alright."

"No fucking shit. Where's your mother?" Ted asked Sean.

"She's," Sean paused and bit his lip, "I guess you could say she's dead?"

"You guess you could say?" Ted questioned Sean's response. Elaine raised an eyebrow at the statement.

"Well, she's not breathing and her body is in her bedroom. But she's also somewhere in here, and is she ever armed and fucking dangerous."

"What do you mean she's also in here somewhere?"

Elaine pondered aloud.

"Where's your sister?" Ted asked.

"Um, with our Mom, I guess?" Sean's reply was meek and insecure.

"What's up with this teenager *'I guess'* bullshit? Didn't you say your Mom was dead?"

"Yeah, you could say that, too."

"What's going on Sean? Where's Meghan and your mother? Are they in the fire? Did she start the fire?"

"I think the cat did," Sean replied, "come on, we need to leave here, now. We have to go before she catches us."

"Hold on?" Ted interrupted, "what cat? I thought you said your mother didn't have a cat?"

"She didn't, that's the truth. But whoever the fuck Biddy Magee is? She has a cat, and it's a motherfucker."

"Oh shit, Lainey," Ted said, gripping his wife's hand, "I know now. It's a *piscín-sidhe*, a dark cat fae. Like a fairy familiar, I believe. It gives the witch her power."

"That makes sense. Who is Biddy Magee?" Elaine asked. But Sean didn't answer.

Someone else did.

"That be us, lass. The infamous Witch of Islemagee at ye're service. And this be me friend, Sabhdh," a woman who resembled Meghan Coleman addressed them in a voice not quite Meghan's. She stood in the shadows of the hall, still covered in blood, her hands behind her back. She removed one and motioned to the large gray tabby cat at her side. A large patch of white fur in the shape of a diamond decorated its chest. It rubbed its head against her calf and meowed.

Top o' the evening, hedgewitch bitch, Elaine heard in her head.

"He says hello," Meghan said, translating for the cat.

"I heard what he said. Bitch is it? Hedgewitch?" Elaine said in response.

"Oh my, ye did hear him, I'm sorry, please forgive our patron. Sabdbh can be blunt. It's his character, we regret." Slowly, Meghan inched forward towards them. The sickle flashed in her off-hand. Ted, Elaine, and Sean stepped back in tandem.

"So clever for a thing out of its hole in the ground for so long," Ted interjected.

"Ah, the faithful stooge speaks," Meghan mocked Ted, "ye're not half as strong as my old John, or even Sean here. Or what about Samantha?" Meghan paused, waiting for a reaction from Ted. She didn't get one. Meghan snickered, then continued, "Ye know what James Donald gave unto me before he died?"

"What?" Elaine asked.

"The seed of the First Born. This means the ritual has begun anew."

Ye cannot stop it, hedgewitch. Elaine heard the cat

say in her head.

"Blood is reaped and sewn. Every sacrifice made tonight. All for our dear Sabhdh and the promise he gives us in return."

The cat mewed.

I always win, hedgewitch. I shan't be goin' back under The Mound anytime soon. It continued to taunt Elaine. Behind it, she could see the first of the flames of the fire spreading to this wing.

"Is that so? I might have something to say about that, you little bastard," Elaine addressed the *piscin-sidhe* directly. The flames grew and she knew the time to go was now. "Run!"

The trio darted away from Meghan- no -they couldn't call her Meghan anymore- it was Biddy Magee, and the fucking cat, her puppet master from the fairy world.

Elaine, Ted, and Sean made it out the doors of SummerHome and into the employees' parking lot. Sam waited for them in the Para-Hunter's production van. She slammed the keys into the ignition and turned the engine over. The producer pulled up with the production van, tires squealing and threw the door open.

"Get in!" Samantha screamed.

The shadow of Biddy and her familiar fell down the hallway, behind the glass doors. It stretched out and distorted her figure into something demonic. Elaine pointed at the shadowy images on the floor.

"Remember what she did to the Doctor!" Elaine reminded Sam. The employee entrance remained open. The editing van launched over the speed bump, through the gate, and down to the street. She slammed on the brakes.

In the rearview window, she saw Biddy step outside, still following them, the cat-sidhe ever at her side. She floored the gas pedal and the van took off.

"We have to get off the property and close the fence behind us," Ted said, "the iron fence will keep them trapped inside. I think it's why she started acting out when she got here, knowing she, or the fairy cat, were captive in a jail of iron."

"What does iron have to do with anything?" Sean asked.

"She's a changeling, someone possessed by the spirit of a fairy, and the cat is a fairy, too. Iron kills fairies. Witchwood, also known as mountain ash, is useful against not only the fae but witches in their service." Ted told him.

"Did you say mountain ash?"

"I did. Mountain ash isn't indigenous to this region, I regret. The closest is your typical rosebush."

"Bullshit it isn't. Brannigan Farms makes furniture out of mountain ash."

"Where are they located?"

"They have an orchard. About two hours south of here."

"A lot of good that will do us," Elaine interjected, "we need something nearby, like the iron gate around this place."

"I still don't get how she's a fairy?" Sean said.

"You'd be surprised," Ted said, "Some scholars believe the origins of the fae and elves are tied to Indian refugees fleeing a great prehistoric war, or as traders and settlers who came to England and Ireland. As a result, the first residents of Ireland were dark-skinned. Much of this legend is tied to the Fae, like the names used for them, in particular "brownies," a form of a hearth, or home, fairy. Their name was indicative of their skin color."

"She doesn't have wings and certainly doesn't look like Tinker-," Sean stopped and recalled his mother's outburst with Dr. Al-Mahairi. *She was calling him a fairy?*

"The magical fae," Ted continued, "like what we're dealing with here? They're shapeshifters and take human form. Even in their fairy forms, the fae don't look like that. William Shakespeare made it up for 'A Midsummer Night Dream,' They're far more sinister and malevolent." Ted replied.

"No shit?" Sean asked, truly dumbfounded.

"No shit," Ted said.

"So what do they look like?"

Ted pointed over his shoulder, back at Biddy and the cat-sidhe, and shrugged.

The vehicle's tires squealed on the concrete road.

"Close the gate!" Sam shouted. The side door flew open. Ted and Sean ran to the iron gate doors on either side of the exit. They each grabbed one and pulled them together. They heard a din when the doors met. Sean threw over the lock and the men ran back to the safety of the van. As they closed the door, Biddy stepped out into the parking lot.

She took her time walking across the lot.

The van wouldn't shift into gear. Sam fought with the shifter on the steering column.

"What in the actual fuck is going on here?" Sam shouted, and punched the dashboard.

"It's her. She's fucking with the machine, too," Elaine said and cursed, "Goddamnit!"

It was true. Behind the gate, Biddy walked up to the barrier, muttering something they couldn't hear. This didn't matter, they wouldn't understand it anyway. The words were from the old gods of the fae.

"I thought you said the iron would contain her magic!"

"I did! It's supposed to."

But we're not fae. We made a deal to use their power.

They all heard Biddy speak in their heads. In the rearview mirror, Sean saw Biddy casually open the gate and step out of the property, the cat at her heels.

•

Meghan and Biddy, the cat trailing behind them, crossed the parking lot of SummerHome. The production van carrying Sean Spencer and the surviving NE-PAT team members sped out onto the street, then it stopped, its wheels still spinning. The van's tires squealed, creating a banshee's wail in the lot. Held back by an invisible force, the van remained still, in a fog of burnt rubber. Meg could feel Biddy willing the vehicle to stay in place.

Meghan now understood how the fae magic worked. Casting spells was nothing more than visualizing an outcome. And this power Biddy controlled, to visualize and achieve a goal, was provided by the cat-sidhe. Its white diamond pulsed as it fed Biddy, using Meghan's body as the conduit.

She watched as Sean and Ted, the old man, got out and closed the iron gate behind them. Meg could feel Biddy's will change, and focus on them.

No! Meghan asserted her willpower. It distracted Biddy for a moment, long enough to be released from the spell, allowing the men to jump back into the van. The iron of the closed fence created a barrier and blocked the fae magic.

"But we're not fae, we made a deal to use their power," Biddy said to no one Meghan could see, then she realized the witch was casting her mind for someone, likely her brother and the Para-Hunters, to hear.

Biddy's will forced Meghan to open the gate, but the iron around them still interfered with the fae power, and the van faded from sight as it raced from SummerHome.

Meghan and Biddy watched as the flames rose higher behind them, now fully engulfing all of the facility. The light of the fire cast reflecting shadows across the metallic paint of the cars in the lot.

We need the Blood of the First Born, Meghan heard Sabhdh mew, reminding Biddy of her quest. Biddy tore through Meghan's memories, looking for something.

"We shall have it, our new sister tells us he will go to his place of employment for sanctuary, thinking the iron in the building will protect him from us."

It won't.

"Walking will take too long, we'll need transportation."

Aye, in a steel wagon of ye'r own, the cat agreed.

"Aye," Biddy found Samantha's Forester. In her haste, Sam left the key in the ignition. Biddy turned the car's engine over, and Meghan's foot found the accelerator.

•

The door closed behind Sean and Ted. Samantha was finally able to shift the van into drive, floored the accelerator, and the vehicle lurched forward, tires squealing as they sped away.

"Turn left up here!" Sean shouted.

"Where are we going?" Elaine asked.

"To the only place I know full of witchwood and iron," Sean answered.

"Where is that? I thought you said the nearest mountain ash was two hours away?"

"The trees are. The tables and chairs and beds made with it? They're at the Donahue Furniture warehouse," he replied, "and that's where I work. It's just across town. It should give us enough time to regroup and arm ourselves against them," he stumbled his words, catching himself from saying his sister, or his mother, "the changeling witch and her fucking fairy cat."

"Good idea!"

Across the northeast, a cold front barrels through, racing to meet its mistress's call. It meets a stationary warm front, and the collision creates a circular vortex in the upper atmosphere. This cyclone doesn't quite make it to the ground. Instead, it takes the stationary air and, much like a discus thrower, gets a winding start before hurling a straight line of winds across the waters of Lake Ontario with the force of a hurricane.

This isn't the first time a straight-line wind storm has struck this region. Some years before, in 1998, the infamous Labor Day Storm killed half a dozen people, ended the New York State Fair a day early, and threw the Central New York region into chaos.

Imagine a tornado, but it doesn't spiral around. It is, instead, a seventeen-mile-wide, invisible tsunami of air. It is moving at 100 plus miles per hour and gaining speed as it sails across the flat of what is essentially an inland, freshwater sea.

This derecho, called by the will of an ancient goddess, will strike land on the south and east shore of the Great Lake. Fenton, New York, stands at the epicenter and will take the brunt of the storm.

Soon, anything it hits will play a game of chicken with an unstoppable force of nature. The wind will win the battle of wills more often than not. Trees will be pushed over, their root systems ripped from the earth. Utility poles and cell towers will crimple in its wake. Streetlights will be strewn about, torn from their supports. It will rain glass, like windows in the tallest buildings, like the facade atop the Donahue Furniture Warehouse, will shatter and cover the city streets.

The local fireman's field days will see its last day, as the grounds holding it are devastated by the wind, collapsing the barns and sheds, and destroying the amusement rides.

The college campus is spared any trauma, but the agriculture in the region will be devastated. The Plainview Turkey Farm's free-range shelters will collapse, killing approximately two-thirds of their stock. The college district surrounding the campus is as unfortunate.

The eave facade hanging over the shops in the College Mall will collapse, with the falling debris shattering their bay windows and the rain ruining anything made of paper.

The rains of the storm will extinguish the flames of the blaze engulfing SummerHome, but it will come too late. The fire will have ravaged the facility, killing all within. The firefighters who arrive too late will instead control the *fire's spread.*

Elsewhere, power and cell phone service will be interrupted. The blackout will last for days as crews clean up from the disaster. The citizens of Fenton, NY, and the surrounding communities, are about to be tossed into the blackout of a disaster.

CHAPTER 28: Special Deliveries

amantha's foot remained pressed on the production van's accelerator. The vehicle raced down Fenton's main street. Inside, the passengers could hear the results of their calls to 911. The screams of sirens joined the looming storm and filled the night with sound, while the lights of the emergency vehicles blended with the incoming lightning and colored the darkness. It all sped toward SummerHome. The responders didn't know they were too late to extinguish the fire Biddy Magee set. Or to save any of the residents or staff.

The warehouse loomed before them. Clouds moved past the full, bright moon as it cast its light down. The shadow of the elevator house fell across the parking lot before the incoming storm blotted out the moon entirely. Samantha pulled the Parahunters production van up to the loading bays.

"I always leave the side loading door unlocked in case I get locked out," Sean said, pointing to a smaller door, hidden by the rubber bumpers encasing the larger bay doors. He ran to the door, lifted the handle with the frame, and opened the door. "Come on!" He beckoned the others to join him. They did.

He flicked on the lights of the loading bays. The fluorescents flickered to life and lit up the interior. The cast-iron sewage drains were still separated from Gorman's accident, and the tow motor was still wedged underneath, holding up one of the damaged pipes. Across the empty concrete flooring, they could see the freight elevator.

"The Brannigan Farms Mountain Ash line is up on the seventh floor. SummerHome is what? Six miles from here and she's on foot? We've got like two-ish hours to get our shit together, right?"

"In theory," Ted said, "but don't count on it. The cat-sidhe can move through shadows. I'm more concerned about this storm coming in."

"This place. It's haunted," Elaine said, "the tethers here for the spirits are strong. Jesus, we should have come here and not SummerHome."

"So, it really is haunted?" Sean asked her.

"Oh, yes it is," a tear formed in Elaine's eye, "the poor souls, they've tied themselves to this building. They've lost their identities and become the spirits of their ideals."

"Souls? Well, I'll be a son of a bitch. You mean there's more than one ghost here?" Sean questioned her verbiage.

"Oh, yes. This place is protected by the spirits, too. If we had the time, I could speak to them, but we don't."

"Mrs. Buffett, I want to get out of this in one piece just so I can tell my buddies that this palace is legit haunted. They'll be terrified to go into the elevator." Sean let out a belly laugh and snorted.

"These spirits only care about the furniture and their legacy."

"The rumor is they are Mr. Donahue and Mr. Fitzgerald, the original business partners and owners of the store," Sean told Elaine.

"That would make sense. That's who they were. Now they are the embodiment of this building."

"This history lesson is all nice and fun, but that goddamn witch and her fairy cat are coming sooner than later. We could be chatting on the elevator up to get the witchwood."

"Look at you, taking charge and all," Samantha sneered at Ted.

"Shut the fuck up," Ted replied, his tone turning dark and angry, "I'm so tired of your bullshit. Your Dad died tonight, too, remember?" He pointed a finger at Sam. Elaine and Samantha stood in place, side by side, dumbfounded. Ted had never spoken in this manner to either of them, "of course, that's all you can do, just stand there and stare at me like you're a couple of deer in headlights. I know what goes on with you two, and frankly, I don't care. A happy wife means a happy life, right? If that makes you happy, so be it. Your Dad knew, too. Neither of us gave a shit as long as the work got done. Well, my little cockatiels, right now, the work ain't getting done. Stop fucking around, get in the elevator, and let's get back to work before that fucking witch and her fairy god cat show the fuck up and piss all over our picnic!"

The rattling of the elevator door accentuated Ted's words.

"Come on, let's go!" Sean shouted over the end of Ted's speech. Sean stood by the mechanism, motioning for the others to join him. They did, without any further words. He dropped the bay door and the lock clicked. "Next stop, seventh floor." He engaged the device and the elevator car rose.

The chains creaked and the din of metal resonated as the elevator came to life. A cool breeze whiffed up from the shaft, bringing with it some of the stench it held. Elaine elbowed Ted, who looked back at her in astonishment.

"What was that for?" Ted asked his wife.

"You know," she said.

"No, I don't know," he replied.

The lights went out, plunging the car into pitch-black darkness. The elevator stopped with a squeal and shudder.

"Welp, that's not supposed to happen," Sean said, releasing his hand from the mechanism. It snapped back into place, and Sean regretted doing so. What followed would terrify the strongest-willed people.

The occupants heard a freight train's roar from outside the building, and the car shook violently. The tinkling of shattered glass created an applause-like effect until everything went silent. No one spoke, instead, the group waited for the lights to come back on or the power to be restored.

Neither happened.

A constant roll of thunder grew, and flashes of light lit up the edges of the shaft around the elevator car, illuminating the interior with a strobing effect. They could hear the downpour of rain assaulting the building from outside.

Samantha turned on her cell phone.

"Great, there's no signal," she said in disgust. Sean could see in the phone's light they were midway between floors. Sean opened the folding door of the freight elevator. It rattled as it rose, shaking the car and forcing the trapped occupants to hold the wall. After he pulled up the elevator door, he aimed his cell phone at the shaft and saw a four-foot gap about shoulder height up.

"That's what I thought," he said, "Okay folks, I've got an idea."

•

On the west side of the city, in a townhouse on Cicero Street, Chris Gorman passed out watching television on his sectional. An infomercial selling something Chris, or anyone else in their right mind, would never buy played on the TV. Fast asleep, and still sitting in his boxers and a tank top with a mostly empty can of Coors Light in his hand, Gorman drooled and snored away. A crack of thunder shook him out of his slumber. He heard the wind outside rattling the windows of his second-floor apartment.

Pretty windy out, he thought and saw the weather alert scrolling across the bottom of his TV screen. He shrugged, closed his eyes, and sank back into the chaise.

This peaceful slumber remained for about thirty seconds when Chris was woken by a call on his cell phone. Opening his eyes as little as required, he read the name flashing on the screen: *ADT*. The security company for the Donahue Furniture warehouse. He woke up, shook the cobwebs out of his brain, and answered the call.

"Hello? This is Chris Gorman speaking."

"Hello, Mr. Gorman. This is Lisa from ADT, we have you listed as the contact number for alarm triggers at 2536 Franklin Intrepid Street in Fenton." To Gorman, her tone and demeanor were way too friendly for her line of work.

"Okay. Thank you, Lena. Protocol says I'm to report to the scene. If 911 is required, I'll make the call. Thank you."

"Hopefully it's just the wind," Lisa said.

"Hopefully. Have a good night, Leanne."

"It's Lisa, and you, too, Mr. Gorman." The phone disconnected, and Chris Gorman crawled out of bed. He hit the head and got dressed as he smoked a cigarette, then headed out the door.

The wind whipped at him. He saw the storm clouds on the horizon of the lake, and a loud crack and the lights on the street went dark.

This is going to be a rough one, he thought. Once in his F150, Chris drove across town to the warehouse. He could see the raging fire lighting the skyline.

Is that the SummerHome place? He wondered. His phone's Emergency Alert sounded off, breaking him out of the moment.

A text popped up with the alert. "TORNADO WARNING IN THE CITY OF FENTON! FIND SHELTER IN A SECURE PLACE!"

The rain came down in a solid sheet of water, and Sean couldn't see a damn thing on the road. A deafening crack of thunder hit and the sky lit up.

How close was that lightning? Chris thought before he pulled his truck over to the side of the road to wait this out. Maybe Leah or whatever the fuck her name was at ADT was right, and the wind set off the alarm.

Sitting in the cab of the Ford, he saw the lights across the entire city blink out. Gorman was suddenly alone in the night, only the lights of his truck, and flashes of lightning, breaking the darkness. It seemed as if it lasted forever.

The rain and wind both stopped quickly with little fanfare. Neither of these deterrents prevented him from travel. The tumbling roars of thunder still filled the night with crashing booms, and the lightning still lit up the pockets where it struck. But the storm had moved south and east towards Syracuse, away from the warehouse.

Gorman floored the accelerator and made it to the warehouse in record time. He pulled in to find a van he didn't recognize parked near the service door, and a Forester. He found this to be odd, but not out of the realm of possibilities. The foreman expected a few things when he arrived at the warehouse. Wind damage to the exterior, broken windows, and the like. But as he turned around in the lot, the lights of his truck revealed more than he anticipated.

"What in the fuck?" He said and slammed on the brakes, shaking his head and rubbing his eyes. Because what Chris Gorman didn't expect to see was a half-naked woman leaning up against the Forester with her tits hanging out.

•

The storm continued, past Fenton, losing strength as it rolled over the hills. It achieved its goal, to extinguish the fire at SummerHome. Nature left a corridor of destruction in its wake. Nothing was immune to the damage.

Over the decades, the city's tallest point, the elevator housing atop the Donahue Furniture warehouse, withstood the blows of Lake Ontario like a champ. Gusts of as much as seventy miles per hour were not uncommon, especially during seasonal changes in the region. But a derecho will hit twice this speed with the force of a hurricane, and plow over anything standing.

Think of a small dog trying to lift a leg and piss against the wind in a typical thunderstorm. In this example, the venerable facade of wood and plaster is the dog. Neither fares well in such circumstances. The former is pushed on its side and pisses on itself. The latter will eventually collapse in on itself. All it will need to trigger this is a catalyst.

Like the operation of the elevator.

CHAPTER 29: Blood is Coming

Chris Gorman parked his truck and flicked the high beams on, illuminating the parking lot and the nude woman up against the car. He recognized her right away, or at least he thought he did. She didn't give him a second look or acknowledge his arrival.

"Is that Sean's sister? It can't be. Can it?" Chris asked himself. Meghan Coleman, he recalled, because she and Sean had different surnames. It distracted him from the light show illuminating the sky around the storm's path. Thunder rolled in the distance. He glanced down at his phone. He had no signal, no wi-fi, or cellular service. He couldn't call anyone.

Why in the fuck? He got out of his truck and approached her. A new round of showers in the form of ice-cold droplets pelted down on him as he walked.

"Hey, ain't you Meghan, Sean Spencer's sister? Is everything okay?" Gorman asked. She didn't reply. Then he saw the blood streaks on her and responded in kind, "Hey, are you okay? Are you bleeding? You're covered in blood. Is Sean okay?" Gorman shielded his eyes from the rain with his hand. Still, she didn't answer. Instead, she ran the fingers of her left hand seductively up and down through the gore covering her exposed flesh.

"Yes, it's Meghan. Sean's in the warehouse," she replied. Her voice sounded different to Chris, not like it did on the phone. She'd developed some sort of English or Irish accent since the last time she called the warehouse. A tingling sensation grew in his belly and his pecker stiffened in his pants. Gorman was unsure if this was the result of nerves, or the very attractive naked lady standing a few yards in front of him. He walked over to her, drawn by her sultry appearance.

"Are you hurt or injured?" Gorman asked.

"The doors are locked and I can't get inside to find him," Meghan replied.

"Well, yeah, they're supposed to be at night," he said, slowing down his pace and easing forward with caution. Something was off with this woman. The rain continued to pelt them and Gorman didn't like how this was resolving.

"Ye can open the doors for us, though. We will give thee what ye desire if only ye open the doors," her hand went to her pubic area and shocked Chris more when she started masturbating.

"Woah, I heard you were saving yourself for marriage or something like that," Gorman threw a hand up over his eyes to avert himself from staring at his co-worker's sister fingering herself.

"Open the door for us, please," Meghan moaned, "and we will offer ye pleasures unheard of."

"Pleasures unheard of? Right. I could, in theory, open the door," Chris said, stammering as he spoke, "Yuh-yes. But I, uh, I don't know. I was called here because of a possible break-in. You wouldn't know anything about that, would you?" Gorman found he didn't trust the nude, masturbating, blood-covered woman who resembled Sean's sister.

"We need to find our brother."

"Well, yes, and we will, but first why don't you get back in your car, where it's dry and you won't be, um, exposed so much." His erection continued to grow, becoming uncomfortable. He shifted his legs, hoping it would relieve some of the pressure. It didn't.

"What's the matter? Something wrong down there?"

Meghan said, seductively, "ye want to join us in the car? The back is nice and spacious." She beckoned to the Forester's backseat doors. Gorman felt drawn forward.

"What, what's going on?" He stopped an arm's length away from the woman. His mind focused on how beautiful the woman was. He couldn't take his eyes off her breasts, or the patch of pubic hair. The raindrops dripped down the curves of her body. All Chris Gorman could do was think about how much he wanted and desired her.

She turned and faced him with her arm outstretched. The cold of the rain hardened her nipples, and her ripe, plump breasts poked out of her chest, begging for him to suckle them.

Chris tried to resist the siren possessing him and the fate laid out before him. He felt his body answer for him as his primal urges overtook what remained of his resolve. She spread her arms out, revealing the damnable horrors of ecstasy underneath.

His darkest desires, all he lusted for more than salvation itself. He walked to her, knowing what he would do if they touched. His groin ached, the tension needed to be released. He opened his mouth, his tongue lolled out to the side, and he trampled forward, the lust guiding his steps.

Meghan swung one of her arms at Gorman. The

strike accompanied a mighty roar from behind them, too close to be thunder, distracting both the attacker and her target.

The elevator house, the Haunted Mansion, on top of the building collapsed. A cloud of smoke billowed in its place.

The sickle caught a shocked Gorman in the face, lopping off his nose and most of his tongue. They landed in the parking lot by Meghan's feet. Blood squirted out of his face. Gorman threw a hand over his mouth, but the blood found a way out, through the cracks of his fingers.

Out of the darkness stepped a large tabby cat with a brilliant white diamond on its chest. Gorman watched in paralyzed horror as it swatted the tip of his nose with a paw. Then it sniffed his tongue, picked it up in its mouth, and gobbled it down.

"Oops, cat's got ye'r tongue I see," she said, then she swiped the sickle again.

This time it caught Gorman in the throat and opened his jugular

He tried to scream, but when he inhaled, he sucked back the blood pouring from the wounds to his mouth and nasal cavity. Gorman face-planted at the woman's feet. As he lay there, bleeding, with no one to come and save him, he felt her rifling through his pockets until he heard the rattling of his keyring.

The woman walked away, the keys to the warehouse in her hand with the cat at her side. Laying on his face, Chris Gorman bled out in the parking lot of the Donahue Furniture warehouse.

•

Inside the Donahue Furniture warehouse freight elevator, the car shifted and dropped what seemed like feet, but was only a few inches. They could hear pieces of wood and metal falling onto the roof of the freight car. Dust, unsettled from the falling debris, filled the elevator with a cloud.

Then it stopped.

"Holy shit. What caused that?" Ted asked.

"The elevator housing at the top must have been damaged in the storm," Sean replied, "we need to hurry."

"Oh, isn't that great." Ted quipped back. Sean shined the light of his cell phone up at the car's ceiling. A three-foot gap was visible at the top, under it, spray-painted on the exposed iron, was a number six.

"There's our way out. This isn't the first time we've had the elevator stops between floors here," Sean replied, "Once we slide up through that, we'll be a floor below where we store the Brannigan Farms line. From the sixth we'll take the stairs, I don't feel much like climbing up the elevator shaft any more than I have to."

"This seems way easier than I thought it would be," Ted said, "I thought for sure we'd be stuck inside this fucking thing all night and day."

"Why would we do that? You'd be surprised at what I've had to do in this building," Sean quipped back, "but luckily for us, there are stairs from here out."

"Whose first?" Sean asked. Elaine shuffled forward.

"I'll go," she said.

"Great, now when you get up there, shine the light down for us, would you?"

"Sure," Elaine grumbled. Her displeasure at being trapped in the elevator showed in her tone, terse and monotone with no emotion. Sean and Ted Buffett held Elaine up and boosted her through the opening. She crawled up through and shined her light down as requested.

Ted joined his wife, stepping up off of Sean's cupped hands.

"You're next," Sean told Sam. He boosted her up, and Sam grabbed onto the ledge of the sixth floor with her hands. She slipped an arm onto the floor, pushed up with her elbow, and pulled her body up as Sean lifted.

The elevator shifted and dropped. The ceiling of the freight car fell far enough to bang into Sam's head, giving her a stinger and knocking her out cold. She fell back as Ted grabbed her by the arms. Sean lost his grip and Sam's foot fell through his hands and kicked him in the face.

Unconscious, Sam dangled for a moment, with Ted holding her. Elaine joined him, grabbing her by the other arm. They pulled Sam up and grabbed her by her shoulders. Her head lolled to the side, a stream of blood pouring down her face from the blow to her head.

"Oh, sweet fucking Jesus, no!" Elaine screamed, "stay with us, Sam, stay with us!"

"Just shut the fuck up and pull, Elaine, pull!" Ted said to his wife, his voice stressed by the exertion and annoyed at his wife's doting on her wounded lover.

"I am!" his wife replied, "Sean, push her up! Please push her up!"

Sean's head was in a daze from the kick. Sam's foot struck him in the nose, making him nauseous. He heard Elaine talking but couldn't make out the words.

The elevator car fell.

The iron frame of the freight car pinched the woman's body. It bit into the flesh and bone of Samantha Thompson's back just under her shoulder blades, snapping her lower ribs. The sudden blow sent the air out of her lungs and woke her up. She screamed as the air was wrenched out of her lungs as the two-ton freight elevator ripped the bottom two-thirds of her body away from her upper chest, snapping her ribs, breaking through her shoulder blades, and pulling her spine apart.

Ted and Elaine fell back, still grasping Samantha's arms. They landed on their backs and watched as a dead and considerably lighter Sam continued to scream with no sound, no air coming from her still moving lips. Elaine saw the terror in Sam's eyes, knowing something horrible happened to her.

Ted and Elaine held Sam's upper chest in their arms until she died. Both disgusted and horrified, they tossed the remains of their friend aside. Ted vomited. Elaine's eyes grew wider as the reality set in with her.

"Samantha! No!" Elaine cried out, "Fuck! No, no, no!"

All a shocked Ted Buffett could do was hold his wife as she cried.

•

In the freight car, a shower of crimson erupted, as if a human-sized water balloon full of blood had burst open. The bottom two-thirds of Samantha Thompson fell on Sean Spencer as he tried to stand, knocking him to the floor, again.

The emergency brakes kicked in and stopped the

falling elevator car. After it stood still for a few moments, Sean hopped up, still dazed. He wiped the blood, a warm, thick paste of it starting to coagulate and harden, off his face and eyes. The bay door was still open and what looked like the fourth floor waited for him. He took a step, then stopped.

The mechanism handle.

The legendary shillelagh of Mr. Donahue or Mr. Fitzgerald, it didn't matter, Sean supposed, either way, it was a weapon and he needed one right now.

"Drive a nail through her heart with a shillelagh," the trucker said to him in the parking lot the other day. He yanked the handle out of the mechanism. It came out easier than he anticipated. It felt good, reassuring in his hand. Then Sean stepped out of the damaged elevator, onto the concrete of the fourth floor.

A moment later the car, along with a few parts of Samantha Thompson, plummeted into the pit below.

•

T*he world shifted and warped, and Elaine Buffett slipped into her personal darkness. Guilt overcame her grief, as Elaine wondered if she was abusing her power to say goodbye to her lover and friend. The medium wasn't surprised to find*

Samantha's shimmering spirit floating in the air before her.

Waiting.

But not for Elaine, who could hear the approach of the building's denizens, the ghosts who protected this, their holy tethered ground.

"I'm so, so sorry, Sam, about this, about your father, we never should have taken this case," Elaine said, lamenting with doubt over the circumstances of her friend's passing. Samantha's ghost shook its head, and mouthed the word, No. Then she smiled and embraced Elaine. Hormones of love and contentment flooded through Elaine's body, she felt at ease and knew Sam didn't blame her.

This revelation didn't forgive her grief, and Elaine continued to weep. They held one another tight, tears streaming down Elaine's face. She opened her eyes and saw a pair of blurred shapes hovering behind Samantha's incorporeal form.

The Hearth Spirits of the Donahue Furniture warehouse.

The two of them, what remained of Mr. Donahue and Mr. Fitzgerald, existing as an amicable temporal duo, protecting the legacy of all their mortal coils, struggled to build. Ethereal hands guided the building's workers, ensuring the quality leaving the warehouse was of their *level of excellence.*

They tugged on Samantha's shoulders, urging her to join them. She mouthed a quiet goodbye to Elaine, and flew off, down the elevator shaft, with the ghosts of the warehouse.

Elaine! Wake up! We have to go! *She heard Ted say from the real world, breaking her out of her personal darkness.*

•

Meghan Coleman watched, helpless to do anything as Biddy used her hands to murder Gorman. She tried to make herself stop, but had no control over her extremities.

Meghan, if that's who she was anymore, was having difficulty telling her memories from Biddy's. The learning curve was teaching her the longer Biddy and she were together, the more everything about each of them weaved and blended into one collective entity.

And she couldn't stop it from happening. Each step across the parking lot brought them closer together, as their memories fused and became an amalgamation of all who came before her, of each grandmother, Biddy Magee assimilated through the centuries. And Meghan finally understood why Biddy referred to herself in the plural. There was no Biddy or Mary Brigit. There was no Meghan Coleman, Maureen Coleman, or any of them anymore. She couldn't think of herself in singular terms any longer. They were all as one, every ancestor to carry Biddy on.

Moira Cunningham and Agnes Connolly. Miriam Clooney and Molly Callahan. Grace Collins and Siobhan Clarke. Now nine women in total over a trio of centuries, all conjoined into one mind for their final life through Meghan's shell.

Biddy marched them all over to the warehouse, Sabhdh at their side. The cat mewed and growled, complaining as Biddy found the key on Gorman's ring, and unlocked the door to the warehouse. The pair entered the building, the cat wobbling as it did. Darkness greeted them, but denizens of the dark could see through its gloom as if a high noon sun shone down on them.

This place, this city, stinks of iron, it makes me weak, Sabhdh mewed in protest, *once this is over, we must return to the countryside where I can regain my strength.*

"Yes, my dear," Biddy answered in her voice, "but we need the blood of the First Born to complete the Ritual of Nines."

Thrice times thrice, aye. Make it so. I sense his being some floors above. I shall wait here while ye fetch the prize!

Biddy nodded, entered the stairwell, and climbed the stairs, singing a song. New to their memories, it caught her fancy and she soon understood why her host enjoyed it. It spoke of the night, of lovers, and desires.

•

Neither Biddy nor Sabhdh or any of the ancestral souls living within Meghan Coleman's mind, saw the shimmering figures hiding in the shadows. Unable to see the other side between the world of the dead and the living, how could they? These hearth spirits, bonded to this place by passion, pride, and love- no matter how twisted -waited for the witch and her familiar to split up...

•

Still holding the shillelagh, Sean walked to the far wall and opened a steel door. The stale smell of the stairwell filled the air. He climbed four flights of stairs up two floors to the sixth, where he hoped to find Ted and Elaine. Sean opened the door and imagined he must look rather horrifying, covered in Samantha's blood, holding a wooden club. But Sean realized it was pitch black, making his concern moot.

"Hello? Ted? Elaine? It's Sean," he announced. A cell phone light came to life and he saw the couple huddled up against a wall of Lazy Boy recliners. He could see the remains of Samantha next to them and averted his eyes, not wanting to see any more of it. "Come on, this way!" He urged them to join him, and they did.

"Thank God you're okay, Sean," Ted said, guiding a trembling Elaine with him.

"Tell me about it. Is Elaine alright?"

"She's shaken up some," Ted replied.

"I'll be fine," the woman assured both of her companions.

"Alrighty then. After you. We're going up one floor," Sean said, holding the door open for his companions with one arm and beckoning them with the other.

As a group, the trio walked up the concrete steps, over two flights of stairs. Rust flaked off the iron handrails as they moved together. The seventh-floor door opened up to reveal more darkness and the smell of fresh-cut wood mixed with the chemical smell of new fabric.

Sean held it open for Ted and Elaine, and as he closed it behind him, he thought he heard something in the stairwell. He stopped the door, cocked his head, and concentrated.

There it was, unmistakable. Rising from the lowest floor, he heard his sister, singing 'Because the Night.'

"Fuck," he whispered and closed the door with as quiet a click he could muster.

"I heard that f-bomb," Elaine said, "what's wrong now."

"I think Biddy and her cat are here."

"Wonderful," Ted said, "I doubt the cat is here, this building is all iron."

"And this floor is all Mountain Ash. Here we go, the Brannigan Furniture line, stored with the carpeting for some reason," Sean shined the light from his cell phone on the storage areas. Rolls of carpeting filled the floor and racks lined the walls. In the back corner, keenly designed hardwood furniture pieces were stacked with sheets of cardboard separating them. The triskelion spiral, the brand's trademark imprint, stood out, resembling a triangle of fiddlehead ferns.

"That's what we need," Elaine said, "that's the witchwood." She pointed at the furniture in storage. Their lights glared off the clear plastic wrap covering the wood, protecting it from settlement and dust.

"This stuff is worth an arm and a leg," Sean reminded them, "a lot more than you can imagine, especially for us, right now."

"And your point is?" Ted asked.

"So, what do we do with it?" Sean asked.

Ted marched to the nearest end table and picked it up. He ripped the plastic wrap off. The small table was surprisingly light. He snapped a leg off, leaving a jagged stump behind.

"That's what we do with it," Ted said, "we make stakes and clubs."

And they did.

CHAPTER 30: Mistaken Identities

Sabhdh paced about the darkness of the warehouse's receiving bay, growling, his hairs stiff from the dangers surrounding him. He walked clear of the iron pipes, beams, and iron grates on the floor. No matter where the *piscin-sidhe* walked in this era, it found iron and steel. The metal stank the place up, and in turn, Sabhdh excreted its bi-product, a malodor reminiscent of the rot of death.

It followed him around, exposing him to those who might be wise to fae lore. Over the years, they stayed in the country, avoiding the city. But the city encroached on the country more and more, saddening Sabhdh. For over three hundred years he'd walked in the light, flaunting his freedom and power. And now, as the technology of man created new magic he could not understand, Sabhdh found he missed his home under the Mound. But to do so would spoil Sabhdh's arrangement with Mary Brigit, the self-proclaimed Biddy Magee.

"A deal is a deal," Sabhdh mewed, *"nay, I shan't return to under the Mound any time soon,"* the fae-cat assured himself. To return to the Mound, to go back under, would be to lose the power he amassed. The countryside is where he must be, free of the changes to the world, free of the technology of men. After the completion of this ritual, they'd leave and be done with the city.

If Mary Brigit is hesitant to do so, he can remind her this is the final life of the thrice times thrice promised, and a new arrangement must be made sooner than later. Sabhdh possessed no qualms over abandoning Mary Brigit after their business was completed. The fae was confident he'd be able to find a new suitor, ambitious for power, to tether to.

Yes, Sabhdh the *piscín-sidhe*, covered all of his options with and without the assistance of Mary Brigit, and all of the possible outcomes, like a chess master.

What he didn't expect was to be attacked.

•

iddy sang her new song and as her voice bounced off the concrete of the rising stairs and resonated, she noted something peculiar about it. She heard the song before, over three hundred years ago, on a summer morning when she was still Mary Brigit Dunbar. The night she discovered Sabhdh. Biddy knew this, another omen like the arrival of John Magee's specter meant the circle was now complete. This life, Meghan Coleman, would be her last.

But not if we capture the First Born, the collective within her reminded Biddy between verses, *we can start the rite anew. Live or die, he is the answer.* Biddy nodded as she belted out the chorus and slowly ascended the stairs.

A din of metal, Biddy's most recent memories recognized it as the opening and closing of a fire door, caught her attention.

He is close, we must follow!

Biddy Magee hurried up the steps. She reached the next landing and discovered a door, a giant 3 painted across it. She opened the door and could feel no one had been there for some time. No, the First Born would not be here. She let the door close and climbed another flight.

On this, the fourth floor, Biddy could sense a lingering echo of his presence. He had been here, and not long ago. She smiled, sensing him near, and continued her ascent.

•

Precipitated by nothing, the blow came from behind Sabhdh, striking him in his testicles. Pain, on a level the fae hadn't felt in a millennia, coursed through its being. What shocked the *piscin-sidhe* more was a stark realization. Someone, *something*, could cause it pain.

But how?

Rolling laughter erupted, it bounced off the walls of the receiving dock, creating an echoing cacophony. Unable to stand in place, Sabhdh walked, bowlegged, and turned around.

The ghostly figure of a man, wearing clothing from the late 19th century, smiled as it continued laughing, slapping his ethereal knee and pointing at Sabhdh. The *piscin-sidhe* snarled and crouched back, ready to pounce at the spirit. The fae knew its claws could damage the spirit's physical integrity, and force it to become intangible when a second strike to his testicles landed. This time it jacked Sabhdh's ass into the air. The resultant pain was different. it surpassed the previous blow with intensity and it...

Burned?

Sabhdh squealed, his pain-filled screech filled the receiving floor with its shrill cry, and twisted around. Somehow his tormentors managed to surround him. His second attacker, another man in 19th-century garb, held a ghostly chain in his hands. The end of it still smoked and reeked of ozone from contact with the sidhe.

Ghost-Iron? Sabhdh laid back his ears, twitching his eyes and head, looking for signs of other antagonists. The two spirits encroached, one from either side, looking to trap the fairy cat. But Sabhdh wouldn't have anything to do with it, and bolted away, his testicles still burning in agony.

The *piscín-sidhe* wouldn't get far. A force grabbed Sabhdh by the tail, whipped him around, and threw him into the far wall of the receiving dock. He flew, tumbling head over tail, until making contact with the steel-reinforced concrete wall. A wall he couldn't phase through.

The impact bloodied his nose and broke a tooth. He saw the culprit, a third spirit, this one a young female. She looked familiar, and he recalled her to be one of the interlopers from earlier. He faced her as a living being in SummerHome, a hedge witch in training under the hag's tutelage. And now, like an angry spirit seeking vengeance? She was a formidable adversary for any fae, let alone a *piscín-sidhe* such as Sabhdh.

"Here kitty, kitty," someone said. Sabhdh could sense no humans on the floor, and ghosts couldn't speak. Who, or what, taunted him? The voice sounded far too familiar. Then he remembered who it belonged to.

The cursed hedgewitch.

•

Armed with clubs made from table legs, Ted and Elaine Buffett stood in silence, one to either side of the stairwell door. They waited, along with Sean Spencer, for Biddy Magee to arrive.

They held a surprise for her, one the witch would never forget.

When they heard the doors to the floors open one at a time, then they would hear Biddy singing 10,000 Maniacs, and the door would close. The metal-on-metal contact resonated through the elevator shaft each time. Fearing the return of cell service and the possibility ambient light might bleed into the elevator shaft and betray their position, they turned their phones off.

When the door to the fifth floor closed below them, they stood, unmoving.

"Okay, one of you to either side of the door, I'll be the

bait here. Then you close in from behind," Sean directed Ted and Elaine.

"Are you sure about this?"

"I am, are you?" Sean retorted.

"She killed my friends, what do you think?" Ted said.

"Killed *your* friends, did she?" Elaine scolded him.

"Killed *our* friends," Ted corrected himself, "Jesus, we don't have time for petty bullshit. Are you ready, Elaine?"

"You bet your ass I am. I'm tired of hiding. Let's do it, time to kick a changeling's ass," his wife replied. The trio dug in at their predetermined positions, breathing through their mouths, ready to strike. It didn't take long for Biddy to reach the seventh floor.

They could hear her approach the landing, muffled by the door, still singing at the top of her lungs. The metal of the door handle rattled microseconds before the knob turned, the starting gun for a race they needed to win. The seal of the door broke, and the stale odor of the stairwell flooded into the room.

Biddy stepped forward one, then two steps.

"We see ye, all of ye. Sean Spencer in the machine, the cuckold and his hedgewitch whore, hiding in the dark. Ye have nothing to fear from us," she said.

"Is that so?" Sean answered and flicked on the carpet tow motor's engine. It struggled to come to life, coughing as the pistons worked, fed by compressed natural gas. A hundred and fifty horsepower engine, on a tow motor large enough to lift half-ton rolls of carpet, came to life. The forklift's lights flooded the room, blinding Biddy, and forcing her to cover her eyes with her arm.

Ted and Elaine capitalized on the distraction and took the opportunity to strike. Ted slammed the stairwell door closed behind Biddy. Elaine struck low, smacking Biddy in the chins with a former dining table leg. Helpless, Biddy yelped and fell to her knees.

"Witchwood?" Biddy muttered, "Ye did ye studies, we be impressed."

"You bet we did, changeling," Ted said, striking her from behind in the back of the head with his table leg. The blow sent Biddy face-first into the floor. She spit out a mouthful of blood.

"Ye're going to damage Meghan's pretty face, and we need it. This hath gone too far, now," Biddy stood up. Words no one in the room should have heard, ancient words full of fairy madness, taught to Biddy from the depths under the Mound fell from her lips, followed by a more traditional curse, *"Trasna ort féin!"*

A carpeting tube shot across the floor from a storage rack. Air whistled through it as the projectile sailed. It nicked Ted in the back and sent him tumbling to the floor. Another flew at Elaine, and missed, but careened into Ted, clipping him in the temple. The force of the blow dropped him where he stood, knocking him out cold.

"Teddy!" Elaine screamed over, and over, as she ran to her husband's side. She slid onto the floor, lifted his head, and placed it on her lap, still weeping and sobbing.

"Isn't that special. Ye've had ye'r fun, children," Biddy said, "playtime is over."

"Oh, is it?" Sean said. The tow motor charged, squealing its wheels on the smooth concrete floor. The tines were raised to their midpoint and pointed at Biddy. Sean pressed the accelerator down with his foot and the tow motor sped directly at her.

Biddy screamed as the forklift drove into her, wedging and trapping her between the forks. Sean flew forward in the seat and banged his head on the roll bar as the forks drove into the concrete wall. Metal twisted and scraped on stone and rock while dust and smoke filled the seventh floor.

The lights from the tow motor filtered through the smog. Blood dripped down Sean's face and formed a pool on the forklift's floorboard. Dazed, he looked up to find himself face to face with the witch.

"A crow's curse on ye!" Biddy screamed. Sean fumbled around for the shillelagh but couldn't find it. To their side, he saw Elaine, still tending to her unconscious husband in almost a catatonic state as tears poured down her cheeks. Neither of them would be of any help.

Then he knocked into something and realized what it was. Sean's hand grasped the shaft of the shillelagh. He thrust it forward into Biddy's exposed chest, stabbing at her with it.

"No, fuck you, changeling!" Sean screamed back. His confidence ran out when he noticed something.

The shillelagh did nothing, not a single fucking thing.

Biddy laughed as she pushed it away and the club listed in Sean's grip. She laughed some more, and Sean realized it wasn't a single voice laughing, it was a half dozen or more. She slipped out under the forks of the lift.

"Is that what ye thinks? We be a changeling? Ye keep throwing that word about like y'all know what it means, but ye don't." Biddy laughed. "Oh, heaven's no. We told ye before, we be no changeling and we don't be fae, do we ladies?" A chorus of laughter and taunting "No's" came out of Biddy's mouth. This included a few voices Sean recognized as his mother's and sister's.

"Then what the fuck are you?" Sean asked.

"Ye can continue to call us a witch if ye like. We've grown fond of that title. It has power over ignorant men and women. But truth be told, we are simpler. We are someone, or someones, who want to live forever, and nothing more. We struck a deal, ye see, with an old god from under the Mound, and our benefactor feeds us his fae magic."

"Who's that? The fairy cat?"

"The fairy cat? Did you really call him a fairy cat, like he was some fairy godmother or something?" Another round of laughter emanates from the myriad voices inhabiting Biddy's being.

"What's so funny? I'm right, aren't I?" He glanced over to Ted and Elaine, and nothing changed. Ted still lay across Elaine's lap and she still stared off at nothing. *What are they waiting for?* Sean wondered to himself as Biddy continued to gab.

"We laugh," Biddy shook her head, laughing, "We guess ye'd be correct in ye'r assumption. Some have called him the Divil, but we've seen him manifest as many things, from a cat, or to a squid. It doesn't matter what form, he takes, we use his dark power for our bidding."

"What do you want with me?"

"Ye be the First Born."

"And what does that mean?"

"We need ye'r blood," Biddy stopped talking. She swiped at Sean with the sickle.

And the building shook in response.

CHAPTER 31: Reaped

Awashed in the black and white world of her personal darkness, Elaine Buffett observed the unfolding action from a different perspective. In this nether realm Ted, unconscious but alive, rested on Elaine's lap. A pulsing, colorless umbra surrounded Sean Spencer. Elaine had never seen an aura of this magnitude and it fascinated her.

But Meghan, or Biddy- yes she was Biddy now- greeted Elaine with a morphing kaleidoscope displaying each of Biddy Magee's nine lives. A shimmering tether of intangible plasma grew from the witch and disappeared into the floor. The mystical line connected Biddy and her host of personas to their fae benefactor. It flickered as the power, weakened by the building's iron, ebbed and flowed between them.

Elaine stood and saw her body remain in place. She experienced a brief moment of anxiety and vertigo as her mind adjusted to the dysphoria of being incorporeal.

Am I dead? Elaine pondered, then realized this was not the case. Her body remained, still and breathing, her heart beating. She could still 'feel' what her body felt, from the pressure of Ted on her thigh to the scratch she received from the furry cat. No, Elaine's astral form stepped out of her mortal coil and could move about her personal darkness.

The tether, connecting Biddy's host to their benefactor, caught Elaine's attention. If the cat could strike her, as it did earlier in the day, then she could strike the cat.

Can I pass through solid objects? She wondered for a moment, then realized it must be so because she rose through Ted's body only moments before. She double-checked her discovery and walked into and through the wall bordering the stairwell, then back into the seventh floor, unabated.

Satisfied, Elaine followed the fairy tether, being careful not to touch it as she passed through the floors. When she reached the fourth floor, Samantha Thompson's ghost stopped before her.

How are you here? Sam's spirit mouthed.

"I guess it's something I could always do," *Elaine*

replied, her words audible.

I can hear you.

"I see that, they say you learn something new every day. After the bullshit I've been through in the last twenty-four fucking hours, I must've won the learning experience lottery," *Elaine noticed Sam laughing at her joke. Some things will never change, Elaine surmised. Like the things, she found most attractive about her former lover and business partner. Sincerity transcends death, and this makes love immortal.*

They embraced and kissed each other deeply. Then Elaine took Samantha's hand, and the duo followed the mystic tether to its source. Upon arriving on the first level, much to Elaine's delight and surprise, she discovered the warehouse's hearth spirits already having a field day tormenting the piscin-sidhe. Samantha joined her spiritual brethren, grabbed the fae cat by its tail, and threw him into a wall.

"Here, kitty, kitty," *Elaine said, her astral form hidden within the wall.*

·

"Kitty want to play? Here, kitty, kitty!" Elaine Buffett's disembodied voice continued to taunt Sabhdh. He assumed her to be hiding from him with some sort of magic, which was somewhat true. His white diamond pulsed as he used his powers to find the person speaking. It didn't work. The iron in the building weakened him too much.

Show thyself, hedgewitch! The fairy cat mewed in frustration.

"And why would I ruin the fun we're going to have and do that?"

What do ye mean? He watched as the trio of ghosts converged on him.

"Now!" Elaine commanded. The trio of ghosts grabbed Sabhdh. He fought back with all his might. His feline body twisted and squirmed, his claws scratching and his teeth biting. But he couldn't escape the ghosts' spiritual grasps.

Elaine shimmered through the wall and appeared, standing by the broken cast iron pipes, still held aloft by a damaged forklift. The exposed pipe opening beckoned them. The cat continued its vain battle against its captors, not knowing what they planned to do with him.

"A few things can kill a fae in the mortal world," Elaine said as the ghosts neared her with their charge in hand, "the death of their mortal foil, for example, but this one has found a way around that. So, we're left with one of the old standbys, iron."

The fae's imminent fate settled in, and he understood fear. They planned to imprison him in these iron pipes. Sabhdh mewed and growled curses at Elaine in tongues older than the Gaelic words used to describe his ilk. This did nothing to intimidate them.

He changed tactics at the last moment, promising life anew for the dead and immortality to Elaine, as he'd done with Mary Brigit Dunbar so many, many years ago. None of this swayed the ghosts or the medium visiting the nether realm she called her *personal darkness*.

With Elaine's assistance, Samantha's spirit stuffed the gray tabby cat into the pipe. It sizzled on contact, bringing a shrieking wail from the *piscín-sidhe*. His white diamond, normally brilliant and white, faded to gray and disappeared into his coat.

Free me and together forever ye and she shall be! Sabhdh made one last frantic plea to Elaine and Samantha. They both turned away.

Metal creaked and the building shook as the hearth spirits of the Donahue Furniture warehouse sealed the iron pipes back together, cutting the ethereal tether connecting Sabhdh to Biddy Magee's host.

The sickle held tight in Biddy's fist, almost seemed to move in slow motion at Sean. He watched it cut through the air, flakes of blood falling off it. Then an urge flooded him, to throw his arm up to block, and he did. The blade didn't strike his arm, instead, he blocked the sickle with the shillelagh.

The sickle bit into the club. Sean twisted his wrist and the sickle broke free of Biddy's grip. It bounced across the floor, disappearing under the rack of carpeting. Sean pushed her away and hopped out of the forklift, dropping the club on the floorboard of the tow motor.

"Fuck you!" Sean screamed at her as the naked woman stumbled back.

"No!" She screamed in response, "No, it can't be! Sabhdh! Sabhdh! Where are you? Sabhdh!" Tears burst from her eyes, and fell to the floor, weeping and sobbing.

"It looks like someone fucked around with shit they shouldn't have and found out what the consequences are," Elaine Buffett said, catching Sean off guard, "shit like, I don't know, dark fucking fairies."

"Elaine! Look!" Sean said to her, "She's not a changeling! She never was."

"Oh, I know darling," Elaine replied, "and right now

she's kinda nothing."

"What do you mean?"

"What I mean is we were able to imprison her familiar in an iron prison. I cut him off from his power while you had her distracted."

"Huh? You've been here with me the whole time."

"That's right, I have been," Elaine winked at Sean, then slapped Ted in the face, "wake up Teddy, it's over." Ted Buffett slowly came to his wits and opened his eyes. A confused Ted listened while Elaine filled him in, reminding her husband why they came here.

Sean approached who he now hoped was his sister, crying in a heap on the floor.

"Meghan?" Sean said.

"Sean?" She replied, in her voice.

"Is it really you, Meghan?"

"Yes, yes it's me, big brother. It's me. Mom's dead?" She asked, tears still streaming down her face. Sean nodded. He helped her stand and they embraced, holding each other for a few minutes.

"I can't believe mom is dead and all of this happened, like none of it's real like it's one of those dreams you were having."

"It's crazy, Sean, just crazy, can we get out of this place?" Meghan asked.

"Sure, come on Ted, come on Elaine, we need to get

authorities here for Sam if any can respond."

"Can't believe we almost lost you tonight, too. You're very important to us," Meghan said. Sean stopped walking. So did Ted and Elaine.

•

*T*rapped within the pipe, wracked with pain, Sabhdh withered with each step he took. Unable to phase through the wrought iron, the fairy cat's only recourse was to seek a way out of the labyrinth. Cut off from the energy Biddy and her host fed him, the piscín-sidhe knew he would starve to death before finding an exit from this iron hell. Gods, too, will die, if they do not have some form of sustenance.

He hoped Biddy might be clever enough to elude capture or death at the hands of the hedgewitch. After a millennia trapped under The Mound, Sabhdh's experiences taught him hope was futility at its finest. As crafty as Biddy or any of her hosts might be, Sabhdh knew her hubris.

Pride.

Pride, the greatest of sins before the Christian God, wouldn't let her do the smart thing. Pride will expose her- no, them- as it did when she first was caught all those years ago. It wasn't until her mother died, denying Biddy as her daughter, that the witch took a blow to her pride. It almost put an end to his freedom then, and it certainly did this time around.

But this was worse than being Mound-bound. This hell was inescapable, and lined with shite. The buildings of men do not last forever, Sabhdh knew this to be true. Crawling through the iron would sap his strength faster. But hibernating? Something he'd not done since Ireland, not since Biddy first freed him from the barrow.

Sabhdh curled into a ball in a nest of crap, careful to avoid contact with the iron of the pipe, and went to sleep until the day he might be free again.

•

"What did you say?" Elaine interjected after Meghan spoke.

"What? My brother is special, that's all."

"No, the pronouns you used?" The medium said and took her husband's hand, backing away from Sean and Meghan. Sean saw this and took a step away from Meghan.

"What about them?" She asked, letting out a nervous giggle.

"Yeah, Meg, what about them?" Sean pushed the

issue.

Meghan's laughter stopped.

"Ye'r not easy to deceive, are ye?" Meghan said, her voice warbling, shifting from her own to *theirs* and Biddy Magee's Irish brogue. "We suppos'd the First Born'd be clever. It's why ye be so special. We need not be tethered to our familiar to work the magic, fools. In three hundred years we've learned a bit."

"I'm sure you have," Elaine said, "how about we don't give you an opportunity to show us any more of your tricks?"

Ted threw a table leg at Meghan/Biddy. It hit her in the face, smashing her nose in. Blood smeared across her face. The witch wobbled, dazed by the blow while the table leg slid across the floor and fell down the elevator shaft.

"You forgot you're surrounded by witchwood here," Ted said as he threw an end table at her. It cracked against her back, sending her stumbling backward, nearly falling in the open elevator shaft.

She dropped to a knee, screeching in agony. Blood dripped down Biddy Magee's face, pooling on the floor in front of her.

Sean jumped back into the cab of the forklift. It turned over on the first try. Sean jammed the gears in reverse. Metal and stone screeched as the tow motor pulled the forks out from the wall, the shrill squeal of the tires. He watched as gray smoke surrounded the tines, pulling the metal spikes free of the wall.

The smoke swirled and Sean saw a face form, with wizened features, a bulbous nose, and mutton chops. It mouthed words Sean knew.

"Drive a nail through her heart with a shillelagh!" Sean now understood. He jammed the club into the tow motor's accelerator and leaped off the machine. Sean watched as the smokey face worked with the forklift's engine to eject it from the wall. Once free, it shot backward at almost thirty miles an hour, slamming into Biddy as she stood up.

"Go fuck yourself!" Sean shouted.

The impact sent her flying in the air and into the elevator housing. She smacked into the far wall before gravity pulled her down the elevator shaft. The tow motor listed off the edge, its rear wheels still spinning.

"No!" Biddy Magee screamed as she fell forward and hit her face on the forklift's rear. She tumbled through the shaft, arms and legs flailing. Four stories later she landed face-first on the mountain ash table leg. The witchwood pierced through her midsection and stuck out her back. Biddy twitched once as the air left her lungs. Her arms and legs fell limp.

The tow motor teetered, then fell down the shaft. It

landed on the bottom with a roar.

Biddy Magee, formerly Meghan Coleman, and once known as Mary Brigit Dunbar, died.

Sean ran to the elevator and looked over the edge of the shaft. His sister's body lay underneath the wreckage of the forklift, impaled and crushed. Tears fell from his eyes.

Ted and Elaine walked over to him, and put their arms around him. The exhaust of the tow motor created a thick fog. It spread across the floor, and into the elevator shaft, obscuring the carnage below. But it didn't hide the stench of rot and death seeping up from the depths of the shaft.

"I know it doesn't seem like it now, but you done good, son. You done good," Ted said, not sure what to say to a person who lost his mother and sister on the same day.

•

Elaine found she no longer needed to fall into a trance to view her personal darkness. The medium could see through the smoke to the otherside as easily as one with bifocals shifts between magnifications. The host of spirits once known as Biddy Magee fled the realm of the living, and moved on to the next, hurling curses at the living as they dissipated into the nether.

Mary Brigit came first. Then Grace Callahan and Agnes Collins, Siobhan Clarke and Peggy Connolly. Molly Callahan and Miriam Clooney. Of course, Moira and Maureen, and finally Meghan. All of them swirling about, like ethereal moths, disappearing one by one.

When the last of the witch blinked away, Elaine sighed in relief. The medium looked forward to later when she and Ted would make love, and sleep in the same bed for the first time in a decade.

•

"Yes, for once my husband says the right thing," Elaine said. She winked at her husband, and squeezed Sean's hand, assuring him this was over, "and so did you."

A tear trailing down his cheek, Sean Spencer squeezed back.

CHAPTER 32: ...and Sewn

Six Months Later...

"Yessir, and thank you, again. This has been some experience, let me tell you, Detective Mitchell," Sean Spencer said, speaking into his telephone.

"And again, I'm very sorry about your sister and your mother. Tragic losses," the Detective added.

"I'm just happy to be back to work, and hey, a promotion at the warehouse was welcome."

"It's the least they could do after what happened that night. You helped save some lives. Okay, enough of this, I've got a missing person's case to look into, some guy never came home from karaoke a week ago. Be well, and be safe."

"Alrighty, Detective, I will, thanks!" Sean said and disconnected the call. He didn't want to remember anything more about the night in question than he needed to.

After a long morning giving statements to the police

and an attorney or two regarding the events surrounding SummerHome and the Donahue Furniture Warehouse, Ted and Elaine Buffett had returned to their rooms at the Super 8-Motel and Sean Spencer drove home. He later learned the Buffetts shared the same bed for the first time in a decade.

Their mutual agreement to omit any trace of supernatural forces from the narrative likely assisted. The derecho helped them create a new narrative, one painted Sean as a hero, rescuing the others from a warehouse during a ghost hunt taken over by a natural disaster.

Now, Sean sat alone in his bedroom in their family's house; half a year away from the funerals and the tears he cried burying his mother and sister. As alien as it felt since the summer, this bed was still his personal Elysium and sanctuary. The aches and pains assaulting his body and emotions faded away under the blankets.

He slept through the night for the first time in months, and though his body rested, his brain did not. The organ shimmered with activity throughout his slumber. When he woke the following morning, a remarkable epiphany struck Sean: he remembered his dreams. When he got to the warehouse today, the guys would get a kick out of this, he was sure.

It fascinated him, how the images lingered the

longest, shimmering in his mind's eye. They'd fade, then return into focus. He saw a field and a bed of flowers. A taste of salt lingered in the air, which he found curious, then Sean recalled...

It was raining.

ACKNOWLEDGEMENTS

SummerHome is my first full length novel. But things like this take a village. It wouldn't exist without the workshops I take with Garrett Cook (who also edited this piece). I appreciate Chris Meekings, a fellow student in these classes, for giving me plenty of input on the first third of the story. Huge shout out to the incredible Lynne Hansen, who's cover art once again had a connection to my WIP. And many thanks to Tim Murr at St. Rooster Books, who expected a sequel to last year's THE GOD PROVIDES and got a haunted nursing home book instead. Thanks to my wife for working as a CNA 20 years ago, wiping asses and dealing with dirty old men. Without her experiences, I wouldn't have this.

Why?

Because the story for SummerHome comes directly from experiences I've had in my own life, and many of the non-supernatural incidents are true-ish. The name of the facility is derivative of a nursing home my mother wired at for s short time when I was a child, called Sunnyside. When I first met wife nearly a quarter century ago, I was working in the alleged haunted warehouse for Dunk and Bright furniture, and she worked as a CNA at Westside Manner, an assisted living facility. The Haunted Mansion still stands atop the abandoned Penfield Manufacturing building on the north side of Syracuse.

On the surface, SummerHome uses magic to show how Alzheimer's can have a negative impact on a family.

After witnessing Christine Morgan's social media posts on the trials of managing her mother's battle with Alzheimer's, I saw how it impacted her, at least that which she shared with us. And most of it wasn't pretty. There were moments of triumph, when her Mom has had good days, and Christine, who is so damn good at articulating her feeling on the page, has me cheering out loud when this happens.

The rollercoaster of emotions made me think - Alzheimer's isn't all that different from opiate addiction. They're both diseases first and foremost. Both have an immediate effect on those closest the afflicted. And both can tear a family apart. I have run out of digits on my body to count the number of friends I've lost to heroin in the last 5 years, let alone the last 20. SummerHome isn't only about Alzheimer's. It's just as much about any disease (or addiction) that can cripple not only its victim, but their friends and family.

Thomas R Clark
June 2022

ABOUT THE AUTHOR

Thomas R Clark is a musician, writer, and podcast producer & engineer. He is the author of the 2021 Splatterpunk Award Nominated BELLA'S BOYS, GOOD BOY, and THE DEATH LIST—published through Stitched Smile Publications, and THE GOD PROVIDES, from St. Rooster Books. His journalism has appeared in Memento Mori Ink, Rue Morgue, This Is Infamous, and House of Stitched Magazine. Tom lives in Central New York with his wife and their canine companions.

Also Available from St Rooster Books

From Tim Murr;
The Gray Man
978-1799252177
Lose This Skin; Collected Short Works 1994-2011
978-1530351633
Conspiracy of Birds/Hounds of Doom
978-1516920631
City Long Suffering
978-1519588074
Motel on Fire; Stories
978-1543039016
Neon Sabbath; Stories
978-1721039708
My Skull is Full of Black Smoke; Stories
979-8680276099

Collection/Various Authors

To Be One with You; An Anthology of Parasitic Horror 2018
featuring Paul Kane, Marie O'Regan, Jeffery X Martin, Peter Oliver
Wonder, Adam Millard, DJ Tyrer, David W Barbee, Ross Peterson
978-1724516787
Kids of the Black Hole; A Punksploitation Anthology featuring
Sarah Miner, Chris Hallock, Paul Lubaczewski, and Jeremy Lowe
978-1072962724
*The Blind Dead Ride Out of Hell; A Literary Tribute to the Amando
de Ossorio Films* featuring Sam Richard, Heather Drain, Paul
Lubaczewski, Mark Zirbel, Jeremy Lowe, and Jerome Reuter
979-8692365187
A New Life by Paul Lubaczewski

979-8615384066
Blood & Mud by John Baltisberger
The God Provides by Thomas R Clark
979-8520227076
3 Hits from the Holler by Paul Lubaczewski
 979-8707581984
Abhorrent Siren by John Baltisberger
978-1955745024
Let the World Drown: An Anthology of Sea Horror featuring Brian M Sammons, Lee Franklin, Jedediah Smith, AK McCarthy, Anthony S Buoni, BE Goose, Paul Lubaczewski, Jeremy Lowe, John Baltisberger, and Carter Johnson
979-8739852915
Souls in a Blender by Lamont A Turner
979-8494735201
Hungry Cosmos by Reed Alexander
979-8776862472
Black Friday: An Elder's Keep Collection by Jeffery X Martin
978-1955745093
Abhorrent Faith by John Baltisberger
978-1955745093
Short Stories About You by Jeffery X Martin
9798438145318
I Never Eat…Cheesesteak by Paul Lubaczewski
979-8440821415
Saint's Blood by Ryan C Bradley
979-8804031863